THEIR EYES MET...

"You are behaving abominably," Rachel told James curtly.

"What did you call me that day? A rake, a gamester?" His tone was light, but beneath it ran a darker thread.

"A fool," she said tightly.

"So I am," he agreed. "The biggest in the world—to fall in love with you."

A slow rage dawned in his face. He glared at her, then grasped her by the shoulders and kissed her long and ruthlessly. Rachel had never been kissed in such a fashion. Afterward they stood, like wrestlers searching for an advantage, then she pulled back into the house and slammed the door in his face. White-faced, a hand to her bruised mouth, she had to face a truth that his kiss had wrenched from her: Her cool indifference to him had been a lie. Her real feelings were very different.

Sheila Holland

THE NOTORIOUS GENTLEMAN

PLAYBOY PRESS PAPERBACKS

THE NOTORIOUS GENTLEMAN

Published simultaneously in the United States and Canada by Playboy Press Paperbacks, New York, New York. Printed in the United States of America. Library of Congress Catalog Card Number: 79-88838. Originally published as *Folly by Candlelight* in Great Britain in 1978 by Robert Hale Limited.

Books are available at quantity discounts for promotional and industrial use. For further information, write our sales promotion agency: Ventura Associates, 40 East 49th Street, New York, New York 10017.

ISBN: 0-872-16589-2

First published by Playboy Press Paperbacks January 1980.

One

Rachel Duncan was cutting roses for the parlor when the silence of the summer morning was broken by the rattle of wheels and the creak of saddle leathers in the lane beyond her garden fence. With an involuntary gesture of dismay and shock, she froze, a long-stemmed red rose wound in her fingers, unaware for a few seconds of the pain caused by a sharp thorn in the green stem. Two carriages passed, halting as they came to the gates of the Park, slowly taking the turn into the long drive up to the house. Rachel watched, very still and grave, the wind gently fluttering her plain muslin dress. Against the white bodice the red rose glowed dark as a splash of blood.

In the first carriage one of the gentlemen leaned forward a little. Opposite him an old lady, in rich black silk, watched him with eyes that saw a great deal more than their expression revealed to the casual observer. She saw, alone of the others in the carriage, his rigid stance, the darted glance into the garden, the sharp-drawn breath as he saw the girl.

Rachel's fingers slowly crushed the stem of the rose. A crimson stain opened on her palm. A few drops fell away and lay upon the crisp white muslin. With a sudden movement of pain she flung the flower down and turned away, her trug upon her arm. A moment later she had vanished into the small cottage.

The carriages jerked forward, under the interlaced branches of the great trees which lined the drive, and in another moment had also disappeared.

The silence settled once more, drifting like golden pollen on the summer wind.

"Frenchies! The Frenchies are coming!" A boy ran barefoot through the dust of a village street, his shirt flapping open over faded blue breeches.

Doors flew open, heads popped out of windows, like maggots out of peas, and the sleepy village street was suddenly buzzing with noise and commotion.

The village of Temple Warren, hidden deep among the curving lanes of Kent's most rural area, had not been so excited since the year 1215, when King John, passing through by mistake on his way to Deal, had caught sight of their priest's woman, and, liking the swing of her impudent hips, taken her with him. Before he departed John, with pious satisfaction, commanded the priest to "Look to your flock and leave women alone. . . ." The phrase was quoted in the village many years after the deprived cleric mouldered in his grave, and King John, hated throughout the rest of England, was regarded by the villagers of Temple Warren as something of a comedian, and appreciated hugely.

This incident, their only mark so far on the pages of history, was not almost six centuries past, but unforgotten, when the boy, Peter Ballard, disturbed their peace once more in the year 1801.

"What d'yer mean, boy?" Jake the village blacksmith bellowed, emerging from his workshop with a grimy face, the sweat standing out like glass beads on his forehead and arms. "If this is one of your tricks I'll slit your gizzard, yer young varmint. . . ."

Peter's sharp little blue eyes narrowed, and he danced out of reach of the huge hand. " 'Tisn't then! Coming along the Lydden road they are, singing French songs!"

Giles Baysprit, the most ancient of the villagers, shuffled off rapidly to hide his valuables under the floor of his cottage, his gummy mouth trembling. "Lord preserve us all. . . ."

Jake lunged. Peter, for all his agility, found himself rammed against the wall of the forge and shaken violently. Sulkily he admitted, "They are French . . . prisoners of war!"

There was a general sigh of relief, then a growl of indignation. A few of the crowd offered to cuff Peter's untruthful head for him.

Jake was thinking, a slow process. "Why should they bring French prisoners through here?"

"And 'ow did you know they was French, young sharp-eyes?" asked Toddy Lammeter acutely. "I didn't know you was an eddicated man. . . ."

Amid the jeers Peter said, with a snap, "Acos the sergeant who's in charge of 'em said they was! Bound for Dover Castle, he says, and he says as how you'd better get your fire blowing 'ot, Jake, acos there's a wheel loose on the cart, and they asked special if we 'ad a blacksmith in the village."

"Why, you young batterbrain," said Jake grimly, aiming a blow at Peter's head which would have taken it off if it had connected. "Why didn't you tell me that before?"

He vanished into the forge just as the rumble of the cart began to be heard at the far end of the village. Feeling that the Frenchies were, somehow, his own special property, Peter ran to meet them.

Ragged and dirty though he was, he was well aware that, by virtue of his birth, he was the superior of every man among the prisoners. Grinning gap-toothed at them, he shouted, "Bonjoor Monsoor! And 'ow's Boney today? Pretty bobbish, I s'pose?"

To his horror and amazement one of them, a slight, black-eyed young man of excessively handsome appearance, leaned over the high wooden side of the cart and replied politely in English. "Good afternoon, sir. How kind of you to enquire after the health of our first consul, and I am honored to inform you that he is, indeed, in excellent health."

"He's not French," said one of the villagers, and Peter gasped in disbelief.

The young man looked at them with twinkling eyes. "Oh, but I am, I assure you—as French as our good brandy!" He winked at the little huddle of girls on the fringe of the crowd. "And quite as potent!" They went into delighted hysterics and brought their mothers' attention and disapproval down upon them.

The cart rumbled to a halt. Jake emerged, sleeves rolled. The sergeant took him to the near front wheel and shook his head over Jake's pronouncement. "I've got pride!" Jake said firmly. "No point in doing a makeshift job. I'm not doing work that'll give me a bad name. I do it proper or not at all."

Glumly the sergeant accepted the situation, and ordered his two subordinates to unload the prisoners. They were shackled together, and climbed down in an ungainly fashion. While they watched, the wheel was removed and rolled into the forge. Suddenly, for the second time that day, the village was thrown into excitement. A noisy clatter of iron wheels and the thunder of hooves heralded a carriage. As it swept past, sending up showers of dust into the faces of the villagers, they caught sight of the arms blazoned on the side, and went into elaborate curtsies and bows. Another moment and the street was empty again as the carriage disappeared towards a distant shimmer of green.

The handsome young Frenchman stiffened, his face suddenly oddly white.

"Boy!" He moved with a jerk which brought protests from the men on either side of him. "Whose carriage was that?"

Peter disdainfully shook free from the importuning hand. "That's squire's carriage, o'course."

"Squire? What is his name?" The young man's face blazed with urgency. "Where does he live?"

"What's it to you?" Peter eyed him suspiciously.

The young man took a long breath and laughed lightly. "Mere curiosity! It was a handsome vehicle!"

Peter looked enthusiastic. "Mr. FitzCharles has three of 'em. I'm starting work in 'is stables come Michaelmas. My uncle's a groom up at the Park and he got me the place. I like 'orses, and we don't have the bother of the family much, acos Mr. FitzCharles, he's usually in London. He always brings a lot o' them rich London people with him when he does come, though, and they tips well, Uncle says."

The sergeant came out of the forge. "Here," he shouted. "Get away from the prisoners, you, boy!"

Peter scuffled away reluctantly. The sergeant looked around him and saw Mrs. Waggit standing on the steps of her taproom, fat arms akimbo. She beamed at him.

"It's a hot day, Sergeant. I brew the best in Kent, our own hops, all home-brewed ale in my house!"

The sergeant wiped his mouth eagerly. "I wouldn't say no, Ma'am." He nodded to the privates. "Hawkins, get into the forge and give the blacksmith a hand if he needs it. Jones, keep your eye on the prisoners." With a sharp glance along the line of Frenchmen, he nodded again. "You lot—behave yourselves!" He marched across the road and vanished into the taproom, the villagers crowding in after him, eager for news of the war.

The prisoners had listened with bored lack of comprehension. The English-speaking prisoner with black eyes rapidly translated and they settled down in the dust, their backs against the forge wall. A low buzz came from the open windows of the taproom. The private, chewing slowly on a quid of tobacco, stared longingly across the street.

"Christian, I am parched," said one young Frenchman.

The black-eyed young man smiled at him. "Courage, Gaston!"

A boy ran out of the taproom with a jug. The private took it gratefully and drank deep. The prisoners watched, licking dry lips.

"What I would give for a little good red wine," sighed Gaston.

"Water would suffice," Christian said.

The private drained the jug and returned it to the watching boy. Yawning, the soldier settled himself more easily, his head on his chest. Gaston grimaced. "The swine!"

Christian's eye fell upon Peter who came at a trot when he grinned. Peter was beginning to have a proprietary affection for the English-speaking prisoner. So little happened in his life that such an alien acquaintance fascinated him.

"Boy," Christian whispered. "How would you like to own a gold ring?"

"Gold?" Peter's eyes popped.

Christian fished inside his worn-down boots and produced a wide band of gold, made for a man's hand. Peter looked at it greedily, then shook his head.

"What d'yer want me to do for it?"

Silently Christian held out his hands and nodded at the sleeping soldier.

Peter shrank back. "They'd hang me for it!"

Christian let the gold ring dangle from his forefinger, glittering in the sunlight. Peter's eyes followed the sway of that gleam.

After a moment, he turned, with a drawn breath, and crept away. The prisoners watched tensely. The street was empty except for them. The whole village had crowded into the tavern to hear the sergeant talk of war. The only other sound was the hammering from the forge.

Peter's deft little hands went to the private's belt. The bare little feet pattered back. The large iron key grated slightly in the lock which closed one end of the great chain. Peter froze and they all looked at the soldier. He snored.

Another moment and the shackles were all removed. The prisoners rose and softly crept off down the street. Christian let the gold ring drop into Peter's cupped hands, then he turned and ran towards the direction in which the carriage had disappeared. Gaston paused, staring after him, then made off in the other direction after the others. This way, he knew, lay Dover, and therefore the sea. If they could steal a boat they might have a chance of escape. Why Christian had gone the other way he could not guess, but he shrugged. Each must look after himself!

Old Giles Baysprit, exiting from the tavern to pay a call on nature after an unusually heavy indulgence which, at his age, was more than his inner man could control, saw the French prisoners legging it down the street and let out an eldritch screech which woke the private and brought the sergeant erupting into the street.

"Oh, my Gawd," moaned the private, wringing his hands.

"You bloody fool," the sergeant cursed him. He drew a pistol and fired. The little street rocked with the explosion. The villagers rushed out, screaming.

The dogs, driven to a frenzy, barked their heads off, while the men, red in the face with the heat and hops, set off in pursuit of the escaping prisoners. For the moment no one seemed to notice the one who ran in the opposite direction.

It was not until they had brought back sixteen Frenchmen and counted them twice that Giles Baysprit shuffled up to the sergeant, having listened with interest to that worthy's language when he realized he had failed to retrieve all his prisoners.

Opening and closing his lips like a fish out of water, his wrinkled old countenance illuminated with self-importance, Giles chuckled. The sergeant turned on him menacingly. "What d'you want, you old ale barrel?"

"He went the wrong way," Giles gleefully nodded. "He won't get to the coast that way!"

"What's that?" In a flash the sergeant had the old

man by the throat and held up with his toes almost off the ground.

"I saw un going towards the Park," Giles mumbled, pointing.

"Why didn't you tell me that before, you cheese-faced old fool? Private, stay here with these prisoners, and if you lose another one of them just shoot yourself to save me the trouble!"

The private looked sullenly over his head and saluted.

"Now, you men," the sergeant said briskly to the villagers. "You will have to lend me a hand. Step along lively, now. . . ."

A shrill twittering behind them stopped them all in their tracks. Advancing down the village street were two young ladies in clean white muslins, with white parasols protecting them from the glare of the sun.

The sergeant took one look and groaned in despair. "That's all I needed! Young females—and gentry, too, by the look of 'em!"

Their wide eyes singled him out unerringly as the person in charge, and they tripped up, smiling with an odd mixture of patronage and flattery.

"Good morning!" Then, with another glance at his uniform, "Good morning, Sergeant."

He saluted politely. Relatives in the Army, he thought! What rotten luck!

They were so alike in appearance as to be thought twins, but a closer inspection showed a distinct difference. One had hair a slightly darker shade of honey, the other had a tiny mole beside her right eye. She with the mole had a firm chin and a determined glint in her big blue eyes. It was, indeed, she who asked, "What is all this?"

"Prisoners of war, Ma'am," the sergeant informed her. "French."

"Oh," she gasped, staring at them.

The prisoners, eyeing her with quite as much interest, set up a rude clamor which was only quelled by an offer made by the morose private to club their heads with his rifle.

The sergeant shot them an irate glance, then turned back to the young ladies. "You wouldn't have seen a man like these as you came along, Miss? One's escaped, I'm afraid."

"Escaped?" Both girls gave a little shriek of horror. "How did it happen?"

The sergeant glanced darkly towards the unfortunate private. "Well, Miss, that's a question I ask myself. One that will have to be answered when we get back to the Castle, I can tell you! Court martial, I shouldn't wonder."

The private went a ghastly white.

Giving him a sympathetic glance, the quieter of the two girls said, "I do hope he has not got into the Park! One could hide there for days and not be found. There is so much cover!"

The sergeant sighed. "We shall have to beat the grounds if he has done, Miss."

"How fortunate that Mr. FitzCharles is home," the more forward girl said. "He is at the War Office, you know, and will know just what you must do!"

The sergeant marshaled his search party, and set off, the two young ladies walking beside him, plying him with eager questions.

"Brother in the army, Miss?" he asked the more determined girl.

She smiled. "How did you guess?"

"Saw as you was used to us, Miss," she said.

"Oh, all my brother's friends call upon us when we are in Bath. We are forever talking to them!" She sighed. "Here, of course, we see little of the world, and my brother is in London at present."

"Guards, Miss?" he hazarded.

"The Coldstream," she admitted.

She looked at him sideways, and smiled. "But you are in the Buffs, sergeant! A fine regiment. Our very own! All our family live in Kent, you know!"

The sergeant warmed to her. He began to relate a long tale of his own daring to which she listened kindly, as she had listened so often before to tales told by her brother's young comrades.

"So you live in the village here, Miss?" he finished.

She sighed. "For the present. My parents are dead, and we live with our aunt. It is very dull."

The lane wound beside a green and shady park into which the villagers gazed with longing, their shoulders drooping after their long exertions in the sun.

Soon a white house showed through the trees, set at the head of a sloping lawn. The girls led their companions across the dry ditch beside the road, and over the cropped turf of the park. Strolling about the lawn were a number of fashionably dressed men and women who, as the villagers appeared, halted and stared at them in disblief.

One of the gentlemen detached himself and strolled forward to meet the new arrivals, his dark face cynically amused, one narrow eyebrow raised.

"To what do I owe this pleasure?"

The more forward of the girls said quickly, "An escaped prisoner of war, sir. He is thought to have entered your Park. The sergeant here is in pursuit of him."

"Miss Lucy Duncan, is it not?" Mr. FitzCharles conferred upon her a cool glance. Then he looked at her sister. "Miss Amelia? How do you do? I hope your aunt is in health?"

Amelia went scarlet and mumbled. Lucy said boldly, "Aunt Rachel is very well, thank you, sir."

Mr. FitzCharles looked at her again, with shrewd interest. "I am glad to hear it. And I am relieved that you led this mob here merely in pursuit of an escaped prisoner. I quite thought when I saw this surge of humanity advancing upon us that we were about to meet the same fate as the nobility of France."

Lucy giggled. He bowed. "I am glad," he drawled, "that I amuse you."

The sergeant shuffled his feet. Mr. FitzCharles turned to him. The sergeant gave a far from lucid account of the events of the day, ending with an apology for the disturbance.

Mr. FitzCharles waved a dismissive hand. "Not at all!" He turned to find a footman hovering at his elbow, the glazed mask which normally served to disguise the servant's humanity cracking slightly as he gazed upon the perspiring rabble.

"Ah, Edward! Will you have all the available men come out here to help the sergeant beat the grounds! An escaped prisoner of war is at large and must be found."

Wildly concealing his excitement, the footman departed. Mr. FitzCharles turned to the two girls. "Will you take a fresh glass of milk? We are indulging in country pursuits and should be glad of your advice on what is all the rage in these parts at present."

They curtsied and declined, conscious of the amused stares of the fashionable crowd behind him. Mr. FitzCharles bowed gravely.

"Must you go? How sad! Pray, give my warmest regard to your aunt."

Out of earshot, Amelia breathed indignantly, "Horrid sarcastic man!"

Lucy was looking rapt. "No such thing! He is the most handsome man I ever saw! And such polish! Oh, Amelia, it quite cut me to the heart to have to refuse his invitation, but I know very well that Rachel would hear of it sooner or later, and then the fat would be in the fire with a vengeance! She so hates us to enjoy ourselves!"

"How can you say so?" demanded Amelia in shocked tones. "When you know very well she goes to endless lengths to see that we have a season in Bath every year."

Lucy admitted reluctantly that this was so, but went on, "She is very old-fashioned in her ideas, though. I cannot see why we should not have stayed to drink a glass of milk with him, but I am very certain Rachel would have made a tremendous fuss if we had done so."

"It would have been a trifle forward," Amelia hinted, not wishing to draw down Lucy's wrath.

"It was the most natural thing in the world for Mr. FitzCharles to invite us, and it would have been quite proper for us to accept," Lucy said firmly.

"We barely know him," Amelia pointed out.

"He has known our family all his life!" Lucy said.

"Only because our grandfather was the vicar here," Amelia said gently. "We have never moved in Mr. FitzCharles's circle." Her curved mouth straightened disapprovingly. "And I must say I thought him very sarcastic, a thing I detest. It shows a refusal to be pleased which is not becoming in one whose position makes it impossible for anyone to retort."

Lucy gave her a cross look. "You talk like Aunt Rachel!"

Amelia withdrew into an offended silence which lasted until they had reached the little white house just beyond the park gates.

Then Lucy gave a grimace. "Ralph is here—there is his mare tied to the post. I wish he would not visit us so often!"

The horse, a heavily built chestnut mare with a white blazon on her bony forehead, plunged forward as they slipped past her, and Amelia nervously banged the gate behind them.

The front door opened, and their Aunt Rachel came out on to the path with the new Vicar and his wife. Rachel gave the two girls a quick glance but went on speaking to her guests.

"So kind of you to call. I will look out that receipt."

Mrs. Walters turned her marble countenance towards the two girls and asked, in a deep voice, "Have you been walking in this heat? I am surprized at you, Rachel, allowing it! Their complexions will be quite ruined. Freckles are worse than anything for repelling the gentlemen, and the girls will have little but their looks to recommend them, after all."

A large-bosomed woman with a statuesque build

and pale blue eyes which protruded to give her the appearance of a boiled cod, she was unpopular with the village, who had been very attached to the late Vicar, Rachel Duncan's father, and whose loyalty towards Rachel was expressed in their aversion to her successor in the Vicarage. Too many of them still came to Rachel with their problems, ignoring Mrs. Walters.

Lucy, who also disliked her, said decidedly, "We are not afraid of a little sunshine, I am sure!"

The pale blue eyes gazed at her as if the gatepost had suddenly found a tongue. "Do you intend to be a charge upon your aunt forever? Or are you so vain as to believe yourself beyond the ravages of wind and weather, girl?"

"We have been to the Park," said Lucy irrelevantly.

Rachel stood very still, her eyes intent upon her niece.

The Vicar said mildly, "Indeed? Bailey told me that he had given you leave to walk in the Park during his master's absence. I know he thinks it a great pity that so fine an estate is unappreciated. I am sure old Mr. FitzCharles was always delighted to see one stroll through the Park on summer days."

"Old Mr. FitzCharles was one thing," said Mrs. Walters darkly. "His son James is another. A reprobate unfit to be associated with young girls!" She gave Rachel a stern look. "You must warn them, my dear Rachel. James FitzCharles is not a moral man!"

Mr. Walters protested. "He will settle down when he marries!"

"With this so-called career of his in the War Office, and the dubious pleasures he finds so enjoyable, he would hardly, one feels, have the energy or the time to marry!" Mrs. Walters looked coldly at her husband. "You spent far too much time with him when you were the curate here!"

Her husband blushed.

The succession is assured anyway," said Mrs. Walters. "Freddy will marry. He is a simpleton, it is true, but I have often observed that such as he are often married early and produce large families. No!" She loked grim. "Depend upon it, we will never see James FitzCharles bring a wife home to the Park. He is far too selfish."

"I have never known selfishness to be a bar to matrimony," Rachel observed with uncharacteristic dryness.

Lucy was fidgeting. Her unspilled news was boiling inside her. When a little silence followed her aunt's surprising remark, Lucy burst forth with an edited version of the events of the day. She was gratified by the result.

The Vicar exclaimed, "Good heavens!" A remark which brought upon him his wife's fishy eye.

Furious at the realization of all the excitement she had missed in paying a duty call, Mrs. Walters seized his arm and with a scant farewell rushed him off down the road towards the village, to catch up with the latest news.

Rachel watched them go with suppressed amusement. Then she turned to look at her nieces.

"You have been very forward, I am afraid," she said severely. "I am, however, glad you refused Mr. FitzCharles's invitation. It shows you are not totally lost to all propriety."

"Oh, Rachel, he's so handsome," sighed Lucy.

Rachel's lips tightened. She looked away over the

park. "Go up to your room now, and wash your faces," she said coolly. "You are quite grimy with all this trudging about. You will have one of your headaches tomorrow, Amelia. You know the heat disagrees with you."

Amelia's lip trembled. "Don't be cross!" She implored her aunt.

Rachel relented. "I am not cross, but I am concerned. Think, my dear girl, had you met this escaped prisoner, how frightened you would have been! He must be quite desperate, poor fellow! Lost in a strange country, probably hungry and thirsty, and ready for any wild course of action."

"Poor man," sighed Amelia. "Only think! It might be Rupert!"

Rachel softened. "Yes, he will be someone's brother, someone's son—but Rupert is a gentleman, my dear, and he would not harm a young girl. This man is probably one of the mob who stormed the Bastille and then murdered their King! It is alarming to think of such a person roaming the countryside!"

Impressed by this notion, the two girls retired upstairs, and Rachel made her way into the garden at the back of the house. There she found Ralph Mellows waiting for her, his fair-skinned face flushed by the sun, his dark blue eyes eager. He turned, hands outstretched, but she slipped past him and sat down upon a little bench under the rose trellis.

Ralph gazed at her with such ardent yearning that she could not help smiling.

"Don't laugh at me," he implored. "I love you, Rachel!"

"My dear Ralph," she said gently. "I am four

years your senior, an old maid. How can you be so foolish? If you ask me for Amelia, now . . ."

"Amelia is a child," he said indignantly. "Only seventeen!"

"She is of an age to be married," she said. "Whereas I am past it! I am twenty-six, Ralph, not twenty, and I have given up all idea of marriage."

"Then think of it again," he demanded. "You cannot wish to remain as you are!"

Her oval face was suddenly stirred with emotion. "No," she said huskily.

"I knew you could not be," he said eagerly. "Oh, Rachel, I can give you a home, children, whatever you desire! Will you not consider my offer, at least? I do not ask for an immediate answer, but I do beg you to think carefully before you reply."

She looked hesitant. "I . . ." She bit her lip, then made up her mind. "Very well, Ralph. I will think about it."

He tried to seize one of her hands, but she eluded him, saying gently, "Now you must go. I have so much to do."

Reluctantly, he obeyed, and she stood at the gate watching him trot down the lane on his mare. The only son of a widow, Ralph owned a pleasant house two miles off. His father had inherited a large estate, but had gambled heavily, and lost so much that he had been forced to sell a great part of his land. Ralph resented the family at FitzCharles Park because it was to them that the Mellows land had passed at the auction, and he found their possession of it unbearable.

He had been in love with Rachel for six months now. It had been something of a surprise to her when he offered for her. She had thought herself past such chances, and although she did not love the boy, she was flattered by his sincere adoration, and touched by his stumbling compliments.

In her own bedchamber she found her maid, Becky, adjusting one of her dresses. Rachel sank down before the dressing table and gazed into the mirror wistfully, tracing the elegant lines of her face. She had been a great beauty as a girl, and there were signs of it still, but she knew that time must erase them soon. Her skin no longer had the perfection of its first bloom, and her eyes were no longer quite so bright, nor her dark hair quiet so glossy.

"I am getting old, Becky," she murmured.

Becky, poker-backed and sharp-eyed, said chidingly, "Indeed, you ain't, Miss Rachel. Bonny as ever. I thought this morning what looks you was in!"

Rachel shook her head. "Over the hills and far away," she murmured, her eyes on the blue sky beyond the window.

Becky watched her, her dark eyes angry. "Don't get in the dumps, now!" She touched her mistress gently on the shoulder. "He's back at the Park, is he?"

Their eyes met in the mirror. Rachel smiled calmly. "He comes and goes like the swallows, doesn't he, Becky?"

Becky muttered below her breath, her face contorted by a grimace, Rachel laughed.

"Well, that is old news! Have you heard the new?" She related the tale of the escaped prisoner, and Becky listened with great attention.

"Soldiers!" The servant spoke contemptuously. "You never know where you are with them!"

Rachel's hazel eyes lit with amusement. "Oh, I think you do, Becky," she said wickedly.

Becky clucked. "Miss Rachel! Such talk!" She shook her head. "We shall have to be careful of those girls."

"I am always careful with them," Rachel said lightly.

"I mean now that *he* is back," said Becky.

Rachel picked up a hairbrush and began to brush her hair. "I know you did," she said.

Two

"If I were a French prisoner of war who had contrieved to escape," drawled Mr. FitzCharles, "I think I should make for the coast at all speed, not move inland again, where I must be noticed."

"The trouble is, sir," the sergeant said unhappily, "he speaks English."

The thin brows jerked together. "Does he, indeed? Is he an officer?"

"No sir. Private soldier. But he's a gentleman—you can see that. Probably lost all his money in that revolution of theirs." The sergeant's voice had a contemptuous ring.

Mr. FitzCharles gave him a wry glance. "Quite so. The fact that he speaks English argues for his having had considerable education. Does he speak it well?"

"Like a native," the sergeant admitted sadly.

"A pity! Well, carry on, my dear fellow. If there is anything else we can do, pray do not hesitate to mention it."

When the sergeant had gone, Mr. FitzCharles turned to a short, stocky young man whose dark hair was carelessly arranged above a countenance notable largely for obstinacy. "Odd business, George!"

"Damned odd," agreed George Bellairs. An orphan, cousin to Mr. FitzCharles, he had been brought up at the Park, and regarded it as his home. The influence of his cousin James had had an unfortunate effect upon him. Let loose on London with a small fortune, and a great desire to emulate the career of his cousin, he had fallen into bad company and lost a great portion of his estate in gambling. When this reached the ears of his aunt she sent for her eldest son and charged him to extricate George from his debts, find him a rich, respectable wife and settle him in a career. "He might find some niche with the government," she suggested. "You must be able to aid him there, James."

James had sighed but obeyed. His cousin's debts were settled, a postion procured for him in the War Office and a quite unexceptionable young lady acquired to be his wife. It was as a prelude to the marriage ceremony that this house party had been brought down to the Park, so that the future Mrs. Bellairs might be introduced to the family she was about to enter.

The young lady had been accompanied by her brother, Sir Henry Danvers, and his wife, Isabella.

Lady Danvers was a striking young woman, blessed with a creamy complexion and rich auburn hair, which she wore in fashionable Grecian style, tied back with a green fillet. Her green striped walking dress clung to her body, revealing more than it concealed. "Is not this exciting?" she breathed, joining Mr. FitzCharles and his cousin at that moment. "I did not expect such a stir!"

"You always cause a stir wherever you go," Mr. FitzCharles promptly rejoined, giving her a glance which brought a sparkle to her bright eyes.

George watched them. He had no objections if it amused James to flirt. James was famous for his flirtations. He hoped, however that this one would not become too obvious. Sir Henry Danvers was no complaisant husband.

"Ah, there you are, FitzCharles!" They all turned at the incisive tones and Lady Danvers sighed with exasperation as her husband joined them. A short brisk man of almost forty years, his complexion somewhat more tanned than was fashionable, owing to his deplorable habit of spending a great deal of his time in the saddle, riding about his estate in Wiltshire, Sir Henry had spent some time in the Army before retiring to manage his inheritance. In the season he hunted with religious fervor, reserving for his pastimes the passion most men felt towards their wives. He had married to provide his estate with an heir, and if he followed inclination rather than duty he concealed the fact. With his customary efficiency he had found himself, within the year, the proud parent of a small black-mopped son, the image of himself and all the Danvers portraits hanging on the walls of his Long Gallery, even to a mole beneath the ear, which was a family inheritance.

A year later Isabella dutifully produced a further installment of the family line, but, having spent two years, as she tearfully put it, as swollen as a pumpkin, demanded a respite and a season in London. Sir Henry at first refused point blank, but having been spoken to firmly by the family physician, an enlightened man for the time, had given way at last. Privately, Sir Henry was happy that he had had the forethought to make certain of the legitimacy of his heirs. He was not fool enough to imagine that his wife wished to visit the capital simply to observe the fashion. When he first met

Isabella he had been aware of her propensity for flirtation. She had been the center of a buzzing crowd of admirers, and part of his pleasure in marrying her had been a sense of triumph over his rivals.

During their visit they were joined by Sir Henry's sister, Elizabeth, who had just spent a year visiting her elder sister in the West Indies, and, having failed to secure a husband there, had been sent back to England in disgrace. Isabella had looked at her in despair. A well-bred, reserved girl, Elizabeth had mousy brown hair, gray eyes and a snub nose. Her one beauty was her smooth, long-fingered hands, and her gentle voice, which was rarely heard.

"How are we to get her a husband?" Isabella demanded. "Even her fortune will not tempt anyone truly eligible since she refuses to put herself out to attract!"

James FitzCharles, looking out for a wife for his cousin George, heard of Elizabeth through the matrimonial grapevine used by the match-making matrons of the fashionable world. He contrived to be introduced to the family, threw a shrewd eye over the girl, asked a few careless questions of her brother, and told George to propose.

Isabella, fatally bored by her husband, was dazzled by James himself; his dark good looks, mocking air of amusement when they met and teasing refusal to take her seriously. She flirted with him, danced with him, walked in Vauxhall Gardens with him, and did not for a moment consider what her husband would do when he became aware of her infatuation.

Sir Henry gestured towards the beaters, moving slowly across the park, their voices a distant buzz.

"Damned inefficiency! Whoever's responsible for this escape should be shot. French prisoners running loose around the country—never heard of such a thing!"

James's brother, Freddy, walked up, grinning. "We ought to take the hounds to hunt the fellow down, eh? Tally-ho! A French fox. Some bag, eh?" His smile withered under Sir Henry's glare.

"Country's going to the dogs," Sir Henry stated in a tone that defied disagreement. He turned to James. "Will you show me your stables, sir? Like to have a look at them."

Mr. FitzCharles bowed. "Delighted, Sir Henry." They strolled away in conversation, and Freddy watched them go.

"Bit of a fire-eater, your husband, Lady Danvers," he observed.

Isabella did not see the point of wasting shot on such as Freddy. She shared the general opinion of his intelligence. Reflectively, she considered George. "Will you walk with me in the rose garden, sir? I am told the sun dial is extremely old."

George bowed. "I should be delighted, but I am afraid you must not expect me to be knowledgeable about sun dials. I am a most ignorant fellow, Lady Danvers."

Freddy watched them walk off with amusement, which changed to concern as he saw that Elizabeth Danvers watched them, too, with an expression which made him anxious.

"I am sure you must be much too hot out here, Elizabeth," he said quietly. "Will you not withdraw to the house?"

Elizabeth smiled, her plain face enlivened by a new warmth. She and Freddy had become friends at their first meeting. She was one of those rare people who saw through his surface foolishness and read the shyness and hesitancy which caused it. Her own shyness made it easier for her to understand a similar nature.

"Freddy, I think that not enough concern is being paid to this matter of the escaped prisoner. How do we know he is not a spy?"

Freddy looked sharply at her. "A spy?"

"It is surely unwise to have Frenchmen roaming loose about the countryside so close to the channel ports. There are a great many military secrets to be ferreted out in this neighborhood, surely—I am certain Bonaparte would give much to know the precise details of our strength on this side of the Channel."

"Old Boney, eh?"

She looked at him in reproof. "I am serious, Freddy."

He smiled. "I se you are. I must confess, I had not considered the matter of much importance. I doubt if the fellow would understand the significance of anything he might see. He probably has but one idea in his head, and that to get back across the Channel as fast as he may."

"He need not understand what he sees. He need only remember. For all we know, this escape was part of a deep-laid plot."

Freddy's eyes danced. "Damned if you have not got a most lively imagination, Elizabeth. I hadn't thought it, I swear! George is a lucky fellow."

Her face froze. "I hape he may consider himself so," she said stiffly.

Freddy shot her a searching glance. "It is really

too hot out here. Come into the house. We will look over some albums in the morning room."

Returning from the stables, James FitzCharles managed to shed Sir Henry and search out his mother in her own apartments. Mrs. FitzCharles lay on a chaise lounge, her white hair and pink cheeks giving her a doll-like appearance emphasized by the lacy cap she wore. She was always goodhumored, never unkind and totally idle. Most of her day was spent in sedentary occupations; the writing of letters or reading of novels, and only when events forced her to take a hand did she betray any interest in the affairs of her sons. She was, as James told her, an ideal mother.

She smiled at him. "I wonder," she murmured. "I sometimes think, James, that I took too little interest in you as a boy. You are grown up very selfish and idle like myself. I should have set you a better example."

He kissed her hand. "But then I would not have been so attached to you. I have seen these busy women—they are loathed by their children, whom they harry from dawn till dusk."

"You see too many women in London," she observed. "And none of them worth twopence. If only you had married—"

He stopped her with a fierce movement. "That was a piece of folly, Mama. I forgot it long ago. It would not have done. And, besides," his face hardening, "she did not return my affections."

Mrs. FitzCharles gave him a long, penetrating look. "Poor James. And yet, do you know, I always thought her secretly drawn to you."

He laughed harshly. "Oh, like most mothers you

cannot believe anyone capable of resisting your son. There was no attachment on her side, and what there was on mine is over."

"Is it?" She probed, but his dark face was closed to her scrutiny.

She smoothed out her loose robe, watching him. "She looked very much in health this morning, did she not?"

A flush rose in his cheeks. "This morning?" He affected bewilderment. "Did you see her this morning?"

"Oh, James, James," she said lovingly. "I am not blind, my dear. She was in her garden as we drove through the gates."

"Was she, indeed?" He turned away, shrugging.

To his back, his mother said, "I have known you since you first screamed for what you wanted, and set your heart upon a silver rattle which your nurse would not let you have to play with. You forget, my love, I am your mother! I know that willful look of yours. You handled the affair so badly. . . ."

He laughed, a wild look at the back of his eyes. "Well, let us talk of something else, Mama. Tell me what you think of Elizabeth."

"I have not yet seen enough of her to form an opinion of her," said Mrs. FitzCharles.

"You must speak to her tonight," James said, departing with a final kiss on her hand.

That evening, he bent again to kiss a lady's hand, in the blue and gold drawing room, with its delicate gilt chairs, brocade sofas and ornately framed mirrors. "How do you contrive to look so lovely?"

She gave him a teasing look. "I protest, you have shamefully neglected us all day. I have been immured here, forced to listen to endless talk of horses. I hope this is not how our visit is to proceed!"

With his back to the company, and his voice pitched too low for anyone else to her, he murmured, "No, I did not invite you here to have you spend your time with your husband, Madam."

Isabella opened her blue eyes wide. "Sir! I am . . ."

"Shocked? Amazed?" He gave the slow, mocking smile which always made her heart leap. "Liar!"

She lowered her lashes. "You promised to show me your charming little Temple. Had you forgot?"

"The Temple of Venus can only be visited by moonlight," he said lightly. "I must ask Brown if there is a moon tonight."

"Brown? Who or what is Brown, pray?"

"My secretary. Invaluable fellow. He knows more of my business than I do."

"What a dull name," she pouted.

"Monstrous," he agreed. "But it suits him."

"Oh, unkind," she laughed.

His eyes laughed back. "Have you forgot you were always to call me James?"

Her lashes drooped again. "It would not be proper!"

"Ah, is that what concerns you, Lady Danvers?" He gave a light, contemptuous laugh. "I had not thought it."

Her eyes shot up to his face again. "You are a wicked man," she said.

His mother, watching them, wished once more that James were not so incorrigible a flirt. "Freddy," she murmured to her younger son. "Your brother is being very provoking."

"Ain't he always?" Freddy shrugged cheerfully. "James has always gone his own way and cast the rest of us to the devil."

"I think he has grown much worse these last few years," she said sadly. Her glance moved on to Elizabeth, and she smiled. "Freddy, what do you think of George's little betrothed?"

"A damned sight too good for him," Freddy said gruffly.

They both looked at George, sunk sulkily into the depths of a brocade chair a little removed from the rest of them. Mrs. FitzCharles frowned. What was wrong with George? Was he so reluctant a bridegroom that he could not summon sufficient courtesy to be attentive to his betrothed?

Although Elizabeth smiled bravely, there were telltale lines around her eyes and mouth; a shadow beneath her eyes and an air of strain concealed beneath her smile.

Mrs. FitzCharles sighed. Lately she seemed to be called upon to do a great deal more than she enjoyed. Why were people so constitutionally incapable of managing their own affairs? Why must she always have to rouse herself to action on their behalf?

Sir Henry barked suddenly, "They did not recapture that damned Frenchman, did they, FitzCharles?"

James, straightening his back, said politely that he believed not.

"I still think we should have taken the hounds out, James," Freddy observed wistfully.

James shook his head. "In my opinion he is already at sea. He speaks English very well, apparently. He would have no difficulty bribing a fisherman. Half of them are engaged in smuggling."

"That is precisely the sort of attitude which has encouraged Bonaparte to believe that we will be easy prey," snapped Sir Henry.

James gave him a cool glance. "Why, sir, I certainly do not have men to spare to comb every part of the fields and woods. My park is already scarred from the clumsy efforts of the villagers—they broke down fences and trampled on saplings, in their zeal. It gave them a much-desired excuse to make a nuisance of themselves with impunity."

Sir Henry snorted in disgust.

James shrugged. "In any case, I doubt very much if the Frenchman was ever in the Park in the first place."

Christian Touslain shifted his weight slowly so that he lay on his left side instead of his right, groaned at the ache of weary muscles, and the twitching of nerves in his cramped calves, then dropped his head a little below the level of the branch so that he could see across the park. A little breeze moved the dark layers of the oak tree in which he hid. He had chosen an oak tree because it afforded good cover, and because he remembered, with amusement, that King Charles II had once hidden in an oak tree from his enemies.

Of course, there had been the danger that the old tale would also occur to this pursuers, but, as he had hoped, the English did not learn from their own history.

If he had been searching for a man in such country, he would have used dogs. A good hunting dog would have sniffed out his hiding place in a moment, as the dogs sniff out truffles in the depths of French forests. The English bred superb dogs, but they used them only for "le sport"—what folly! He had almost fallen off his perch with laughter as he watched the peasants wandering aimlessly to and fro, poking idly at the long grass and calling to one another.

He had had a sudden desire to call out, "Messieurs—me voici!" It was all so much like a child's game of hide and seek. Almost it was unfair to play with them. They did not take the game sufficiently seriously. They had no fire in their bellies. A people who play at war are somehow frightening, Christian thought, remembering his French comrades, with their burning eyes and dedicated faces. What would the English do, confronted with such fanatics? A small twinge of compassion pierced him. How could these large, slow English children win such an unequal struggle?

The afternoon wore on, the setting sun blazed on the horizon, turning the cool, shadowy park into a battlefield, streaks of orange flame stabbing across the sky, like flashes from a cannon. Shadows engulfed the light slowly. The dusky air became alive with moths and little, humming insects which irritated and pestered hm.

Then the moon moved uneasily through a maze of dark clouds, appearing and disappearing, suffusing the landscape with a gentle, misty glow which enabled him to decipher the general outline of the park. Around him oak and noble beech were thickly planted, but they thinned out as the land sloped away down to a lake.

Beyond the placid water the moonlight gleamed fitfully on white pillars and a small, circular roof.

Christian guessed it to be a folly—he had seen them often enough in France. During the night, he decided, this would be a good place to hide, and certainly more comfortable than the branches of a tree!

In sliding down, however, he ripped his sleeve on a sharp branch and inflicted a painful cut on his arm. Blood oozed out and dropped down his shirt.

The moon's irregular course made it simple for him to keep hidden. He stayed close to a tree while she shone out, and when she slid behind a cloud he ran, ducking and watching the sky for that telltale radiance spreading at the edge of the darkness.

At last he stood gazing down at the gleaming water of the lake. The white moonlit slopes, the little Grecian temple, were like the backcloth to a dream, giving an air of unreality to his situation.

The moon went out like a pinched candle, leaving a gray wisp of smoky cloud trailing across the sky. He slid past the temple and stood on the edge of an ornate garden, staring at the lit windows of a large house. The windows were open. A sound of laughter and voices drifted out, a distant echo of music weaving through them.

"Oh, mon Dieu," Christian muttered to himself. "What am I to do? I cannot walk into the drawing room! How am I to get him alone? If only I knew which room was his bedchamber. . . ."

Suddenly, someone came out of a terrace door. Christian caught a gleam of silk, the flaring glint of jewels on a woman, in the candle light. A lady said, "It was in the Temple, I am certain. . . ."

"I will make a thorough search, Lady Danvers," a man replied.

Christian stiffened. It was he! That voice could not be mistaken! He recognized it without a shadow of doubt.

The lady turned back into the lighted room. The man walked through the garden. Behind his sheltering yew bush, Christian waited. As the man drew level he whispered, "Bonsoir, M'sieur. Je vous en prie . . . je suis Christian Touslain. . . ."

The moving figure stiffened into immobility. There was a long silence, then the voice said very softly, "I beg your pardon?"

"Oh, you know me," replied Christian. "Mister FitzCharles! We met one dark night on the beach near Calais. I brought you a certain package from by uncle, Etienne Touslain."

Again a silence. Christian could almost hear the whirr of the brain, the hurried assessment of the position. Then the man said, "And so?"

"You will help me to escape," Christian said flatly.

"Why should I do that?"

"Because if you do not I shall inform the English authorities that you are a spy—that it is French gold which helps you to maintain this very lovely house, these beautiful gardens. They will put me in prison at Dover Castle. You, M'sieur, they will shoot."

"And will your uncle, who has so carefully built up his contacts in England, be pleased that you destroy what he has built?"

"It is my liberty I seek, not my uncle's approval," said Christian.

"And France? What of France?"

"I love my country so much that I am eager to return to her," Christian said. "After all, M'sieur, it is quite natural. Let us not threaten or insult each other. We are allies. All I ask is that you help me to get back to France. I do not even ask this service for nothing—my uncle will pay you well."

"And how am I to smuggle you out of England?"

"You use the free traders to carry your information. They can carry me. It is easy."

"Easy?" There was a bitter note in the other man's voice. "You don't know what you are saying!"

"Where is the difficulty?"

"The coast is being watched for you. No free trader would touch you at any price. It is far too risky."

"It must be done, however," Christian said with bland menace. "For your own sake, M'sieur."

"Yes," said the other. "You leave me no alternative, it seems."

Christian laughed, concealing his relief. He had won, then! The sweat stood out on his forehead. Fate had been kind to him today. "What luck," he said lightly, "that I saw your coach go past, and recognized you. I had no idea where you lived —it was sheer chance that I saw you, my uncle's best agent, able to help me escape."

"Ill luck for me, however," said the other man. "We must not stay here. You see that little building down by the lake?"

"The folly?"

"Yes. I will meet you there when the guests have retired for the night. Keep out of sight. I'll whistle, like this . . ."

He whistled a short stave. "Understand?"

"Of course," agreed Christian. "I will be there. Do not fail me, or it will be unfortunate for you."

In the blue and gold drawing room the house party were pursuing pleasure in their various ways. A card table had been set up and Mrs. FitzCharles had lured Sir Henry, her son Freddy and her nephew George to play with her. Elizabeth was seated at the piano, playing some light Scottish airs popular in London, while Isabella, upon the striped blue sofa, glanced idly through an album of prints.

Mr. FitzCharles came back into the room from the hall and crossed to speak to Isabella. "I am afraid there is no sign of your bracelet at the Temple. Are you sure it was left there?"

She rose, smoothing down the fragile, floating strands of silver gauze which revealed so subtly the clinging nature of her underdress. "I think I put it down upon a cushion. Perhaps it slipped down behind it? I suppose the only answer is to look for myself! You men are so helpless!"

Sir Henry was seated with his back to them as they strolled out of the room on to the terrace. Isabella pulled her shawl around her shoulders. "How cool and restful it is out here!"

"The grass will be damp with evening dews," Mr. FitzCharles pointed out.

"As if that signified," she said easily. She looked up at the sky. "A poor moon! I had expected you to summon up the most exquisite moon tonight."

"The moon is a lady," he murmured. "And like all females does not enjoy competition—your beauty has made her jealous and she has hidden herself behind the clouds."

She clutched at his shoulder, pretending to trip. "It is so dark out here. I did not see the steps."

"We are still near the house," Mr. FitzCharles said. "Let us walk towards the temple."

She laughed. "Craven!"

"Contain your eagerness, my love," he murmured ironically. "You would not wish your husband's jealousy to be aroused."

On the other side of the lake, moving towards thick cover, Lucy and Amelia Duncan crept forward, giggling nervously as they came nearer to the house.

"Oh, do let us go back, Lucy," quavered Amelia. "It is so dark! And I cannot bear to imagine what James FitzCharles would say if he caught us prying on him at such an hour— his sarcasm would be unbearable."

"It will be worth it to catch a glimpse of their gowns. I long to see these new fashions for evening wear—they sound so delightfully daring!"

"I could never wear a transparent dress," Amelia quavered, clutching at her sister's arm. "Shockingly forward! I am certain none of Mr. FitzCharles's guests will be wearing them!"

"Do not be so prosy, Amelia," said Lucy scornfully. "Of course they will! These are just the sort of people who create the newest fashion! I saw that this morning!"

"Suppose Rachel goes into our room and finds us gone?" Amelia whispered. "And what of the tales the villagers tell, about the Temple in the park, which is haunted?"

"Fiddlesticks," Lucy said boldly, stamping her feet. "I have not come so far to turn back tamely before I have seen what I came to see, and so I warn you!"

"I'm afraid of ghosts, Lucy," Amelia whimpered.

Lucy pinched her hard, and Amelia jumped.

"There! When a ghost does that to you, you may believe in it. Until that moment, pray, do not mention them to me." Lucy's voice had such determination that Amelia fell silent.

Suddenly Lucy halted. "I see the Temple, through the trees here. It is not so far to the house now."

"Why did we have to take such a roundabout route?" Amelia asked plaintively. "My feet ache so!"

"You know very well that we could not afford to be seen walking up the drive," Lucy scolded. "Do hush, Amelia. You have done nothing but complain. . . ." Her voice broke off and she froze, gripping her sister's arm. "Hush! Are those voices?"

Amelia turned to flee but was held fast. "What a jelly you are," Lucy said scornfully. "Listen! There are voices coming from the Temple."

Amelia gave a moan of horror. "Ghosts. . . ."

"Nonsense," Lucy said firmly. "I imagine we are about to find out how well deserved James FitzCharles's reputation is. . . ."

The village had whispered for years of the scandalous doings of the guests brought down from London by Mr. FitzCharles. Nameless deeds, unfit for delicate female ears, wild parties and shameless debauchery were rumored to occupy these brief visits. The temple was decorated with lewd statuary, it was said—naked foreign females in unspeakable postures, according to Mrs. Walters. Amelia had a sudden horrid vision of what they might witness. "Oh, heavens," she cried wildly. "I shall die. . . ."

"Do not be such a goose, Amelia. I wish I had not brought you with me—I have a very good mind to send you home alone."

Amelia shrieked. Lucy clapped a hand upon her

mouth. "Do you wish to make our presence known?"

At the Temple Mr. FitzCharles turned towards the massed trees, frowning. Lady Danvers asked nervously, "Good God, what was that?"

"An owl," he soothed. "There are many of them in the park."

She shuddered. "Oh, I detest them, those talons, and their staring eyes. . . ."

"You are safe with me," he murmured.

She looked up, her hand clinging to his shoulder. "You do not look safe, James. . . ."

"Come into the temple," he said softly. "Danger of a certain sort is worth the risk."

She gave a low moan of passion. "James. . . ."

He bent his head to kiss her upturned lips, but as he did they both heard a clear, soft, unmistakable giggle.

"Merciful Heavens," he cried, thrusting Isabella away. "Females! What the devil are they doing here at this hour!"

Lucy, stifling her giggles, saw with dismay that he was walking fast towards their hiding place. Amelia, made brave by terror, pulled at her arm.

"Oh, be quick, Lucy—he will catch us!"

Mr. FitzCharles was bearing fast down upon them, his face grim. Lucy gave a great start, turned and ran, her hand knocking against the locket swinging from a chain around her throat. The chain became entangled in her fingers and, as she pulled, broke. The locket flew off. Lucy hesitated for a second, looking down in search of it, but it was so dark, and Amelia shrieked with alarm at this delay.

Lucy reluctantly ran on, after her sister, disappearing into the trees.

Mr. FitzCharles halted on the narrow path, glancing about. There was now no sign of the intruders. He shrugged and walked back. His foot kicked against something. He glanced down and saw the gleam of gold. Bending, he picked it up, examined it curiously and found the tiny catch which secured it. The locket flew open. He read the neat inscription by the faint light of the wandering moon, and a strange smile quivered over his sardonic features.

When he rejoined Lady Danvers she gazed at him in distress. "Who was it? Oh, James, I am ruined if this reaches my husband's ears. What did they see? What did they hear?"

"Calm yourself, my dear," he soothed. "They were village girls of no importance, no doubt coming here for an assignation with some of my servants. They will gossip, perhaps, but it will not reach your husband's ears." His smile gleamed curiously, defiant and mocking. "It will be one more tale to add to the many already circulating in the village about my wicked ways."

I believe you enjoy your notoriety!" she accused angrily. His face was unreadable. "Why not? I cannot escape it."

"Take me back to the house," she cried wildly. "At once!"

"I am your ladyship's servant," he agreed blandly, offering her his arm.

Three

Christian, crouched in the shadow of one of the great oaks, had been an uneasy spectator of the little charade. He had been somewhat at a loss as the drama unfolded, having for a brief moment of alarm taken the approaching figures to be connected with his presence there, only to be amazed when he realized that one of them was a female. For a pair of lovers to choose such a rendezvous at this particular moment struck him as highly inconvenient, a jest by the same droll fate which had given him his chance to escape. Wondering if they intended their stay at the Temple to be a long one he had waited, heart beating, ears pricked for the slightest sound. It would be disastrous if they caught him.

"Mon Dieu," he had observed to himself bitterly, "Why could they not make their amours elsewhere?"

A true Frenchman, his own heart had yearned a little as he saw the ardent, upturned countenance of the lady, her beauty illumined briefly by the moon.

"Ah, la belle," he had said to himself enviously.

Then had come the other intrusion; the giggle, the startled silence and the running feet.

For a few bewildered moments he had himself been poised on the edge of flight, but then the moon went in again leaving him in comforting darkness, and when he dared to peer out again all was quiet. The interrupted lovers returned to the house and he was left in full possession of the park.

He stretched his arms, yawning. The need for sleep was becoming a matter of urgency. He was exhausted, famished, his mouth as dry as a desert, his stomach hollow. For so many hours he had been at full stretch, constantly alert, unable to relax.

Above him the sky seemed to move slowly, as if drawn by an immense hand towards the west, the clouds gray and smoky, the moonlight filtering through like milk strained through gauze.

He leaned against the oak tree, conscious suddenly of a deep peace, partly born of the mental elevation brought on by hunger, partly because for this moment, he was free; breathing clean air not the fetid stink of a prison cell made foul by rank straw and the odor of too many bodies in too small a place.

How could life be so cruel, his future so uncertain, while the natural world was so resonant of tranquillity and harmony?

The silence was shattered by a dreadful cry, the shriek of a small animal in the final pang. His imagination, shuddering, supplied the image of a rabbit in the talons of an owl or the jaws of a slinking fox out there in the darkness of the trees, and he mocked himself.

"Fool, imbecile! What an optimist you are! Kill or be killed is nature's way, and man is a part of nature, so why should he not follow the path of the fox? It is logical."

A sound came again, nearer, softer. He saw a shadow detach itself and move towards the Temple, heard the low whistle he had been told to expect.

"I am here," Christian said, stepping out of his shelter.

The other man sighed. "So you are! What a pity."

Warned by something in his tone Christian stepped quickly back, but as he did so the other man brought up his right hand and stabbed upward at Christian's ribs. The blade tore across his chest, leaving a trail of fire. Christian staggered, his hand instinctively thrusting the other man away. While his enemy was off balance he brought up his knee into the other man's groin. Doubling up the other dropped the knife and groaned aloud. Christian, pulling his jacket tightly around him, ran into the trees.

He felt a thick wetness against his hand. "Fool," he cursed himself. "Why didn't you anticipate this?" Then he knew that he had, at an intuitive level, and had not understood what his instincts warned him against. The path of the fox, he thought ironically. Oh, indeed! His breath rasped in his throat, his weary muscles ached protestingly.

Through the pulsing in his ears he heard the sound of someone blundering after him. He was unable now to see where he went, the sweat was raining into his eyes making him blind—sweat, or tears, he could not tell which. Pain whipped him onward, pain and fear, but with each step it became harder to move. Suddenly he tripped over a tree root and pitched headlong down what seemed to be a ravine, but which, he later realized, was a dry ditch, steep-sided, the bottom full of withered leaves.

He lay, gasping, his heart thudding, waiting for the end. It was impossible for him to move.

The pursuer, though, had been further off than he had supposed. It was another moment or two before the blundering steps grew close. He had recovered enough to turn his face downwards into the bed of leaves in an attempt to stifle the sound of his own breathing. His lungs filled with the moist, earthy odor. A leaf edge pricked his nose. All of his being was concentrated in his ears.

The feet moved closer and closer. Then all sound ceased for a second or two, as if the pursuer halted to listen. Then there was a soft exhalation of breath, a wrenched sigh.

Poor devil, thought Christian. He must be as terrified as I am!

There was a crack of twigs under foot. Somewhere above him he heard loud breathing. He resisted an impulse to get up and run.

At last the feet moved off. Slowly the sound receded. For a long time Christian listened as the other man drew further and further away. Then he slowly slid into unconsciousness.

In their headlong flight from the terrible Mr. FitzCharles, Lucy and Amelia lost themselves in the narrow, winding paths. Brambles tore at their clothes, rabbit holes tripped them up, strange sounds assailed their ears. They ran on and on until they found themselves on the wrong side of the park with a long walk home in front of them, along a road sometimes used by overnight carters taking goods to Dover.

"We shall have to go back," Lucy pronounced,

seeing where they were. "It will be safer in the park than on that road at this hour!"

"I cannot," sobbed Amelia, panting after her exertions.

"You do not imagine he is still hot on our heels," said Lucy crossly. "Depend upon it he has returned to that female long since." Adding, a trifle bitterly, "And I dare say forgotten our very existence!"

"Oh, I hope so," Amelia moaned. "I was never so mortified in my life. To be discovered in such a situation."

"Who do you think she was?" Lucy mused. "Some lightskirt, I suppose." She had not spent her formative years among soldiers for nothing.

"Oh," shrieked Amelia in horror.

"Why do you squeak in that fashion?" demanded Lucy irritably. "Why else should she be out there at such an hour, with a gentleman? Embracing him in that way! I must say, though, I did not think her so very alluring."

Amelia said frankly, "Well, she was, and so you know, Lucy! Her gown was quite heavenly."

Lucy sighed. "Oh, why must you be always so honest, Amelia? It was, indeed, quite the loveliest dress I ever saw, clearly the newest fashion."

"Yes, it was very shocking," said Amelia. "Did you see how thin it was? Her shawl was no protection."

"Did you hear her shriek when I giggled?" Lucy giggled again, with great satisfaction. Then her face altered. "I wish I had not lost my locket though."

"Oh, Lucy, you did not!"

"I wish you would not do that," said Lucy crossly. "You have pinched me black and blue tonight. Let go my arm! It is no great matter, after all. We can find the locket in the morning."

"It has your name inside it," Amelia reminded her. "If *he* should find it!"

"He would take it to Rachel and the fat would be in the fire," Lucy nodded. "We must go back for it now."

"No," shrieked Amelia.

"I know where I lost it," Lucy said firmly. "We have to go back through the park to get to the lodge anyway!"

Amelia was torn between her fear of the journey, and her fear of exposure and punishment. Weakly she allowed Lucy to drag her back among the trees, but she wept silently as they went.

"I declare, Amelia, you are the most spineless female it has ever been my misfortune to know," said Lucy.

They made their way more carefully, pausing often to take a bearing by the errant gleams of moonlight. They had known the park all their lives, but were not in the habit of walking there by night, and it had a strange appearance, silvered and unearthly.

They had almost reached the spot when they heard an eerie sound. Amelia's feet were suddenly rooted to the ground. Every separate hair on her head stood up in horror. "The ghost. . . ."

"Ssh. . . ." Lucy's own voice quivered slightly, for all her spirit, and she caught her sister's hand and held it tight.

The sound came again, a low muffled groan.

"Ggghost. . . ." Amelia stuttered, turning to run.

"No," said Lucy sharply. "It is someone crying!"

Amelia's soft heart winced. "Oh, poor thing!

You are right! It must be an animal caught in a trap!"

"It sounds to be in great pain," Lucy said. "We must find it."

"It is coming from that direction," Amelia said decisively, moving off.

"I thought you were frightened?" said Lucy.

"Of ghosts," Amelia said. "But never of some poor animal in a trap." She hurried towards the sound, hardly watching where she trod.

Suddenly the earth seemed to fall away beneath her. She clutched at Lucy, dragging her down too, slipping and sliding into a deep ditch. Amelia fell upon her face, her hands flung out to grab at the earth. Lucy fell on top of her, knocking all the breath out of her.

"Do get up, Lucy," Amelia begged after a moment, her mouth pressed into a pile of leaves. "I cannot breathe."

Lucy slowly did so. As she sat up her eye fell upon a dark shape a few yards from them.

Sitting very still indeed, she whispered, "Do not move too suddenly, Amelia! I think the wounded animal is in the ditch with us."

Carefully Amelia sat up, pushing her hair out of her eyes. She peered into the darkness. "What is it?" She whispered. "It is too big to be a rabbit. Can it be a badger, do you think?"

"I think . . ." said Lucy, crawling slowly towards the shape. "I think it is a man. . . ."

She bent over the inert shape, speaking softly. There was no answer. The moon, sliding overhead, showed her a pale, dark, handsome face marked by lines of pain, showed her too a jacket fallen open to reveal an ominous stain spreading across the young man's shirt, and, as she drew back in involuntary dismay, showed her the same stains on her own hands.

"Oh," she said, very faintly. "Oh!"

For the very first time in her life Lucy Duncan fainted.

When she came to herself again it was to find Amelia supporting her head upon her lap, weeping upon her.

"Stop it, Amelia," she said crossly, sitting up, and pushing her sister away.

"Lucy," gasped Amelia, "you fainted!"

Lucy conceded that for once Amelia's tone of stunned amazement was justified. "I did not think fainting would be like that," she observed thoughtfully. "I seemed to go quite cold, from head to foot, as though I were drowning in icy water." She shuddered. "It was not pleasant." Then she remembered what had caused her to faint, and asked hastily, "Is he dead?"

Amelia gave a great start. In her concern for her sister she had forgotten the cause of the trouble. "I do not know. I was far too anxious on your behalf to look at him."

"You have no sense of proportion," cried Lucy. "How could you be so thoughtless? He is wounded, bleeding! Could it have been a duel, do you imagine? A combat of honor? But then why should he be lying here in a ditch, unattended?"

"He is more like to be a poacher," Amelia said prosaically. "One of the keepers may have shot him, and he has hidden here until he can get away."

"That may be," Lucy conceded reluctantly. "But he is so young and handsome! I cannot think he is a poacher! What shall we do?"

"One of us must go to the house," Amelia suggested.

Lucy nodded. "Yes, we cannot leave him here. He might bleed to death or die of exposure!" She bent over him once more, her eye tracing the fine lines of his features. "What a romantic face! Amelia, you must go. Run to the house and ask Mr. FitzCharles to send some men down here. . . ."

The young man's eyes opened. His hand shot out to grasp Lucy's wrist with surprising strength.

"No!"

Lucy stared in astonishment.

"Do not give me up to him, I implore you!"

"No, no, of course not, if you do not wish it," Lucy soothed. "But then how are we to get you away from here?"

He lay back, with a deep sigh. "Miss, before you say anything more, I think it necessary to tell you that I am an escaped prisoner of war."

Amelia shrank. "Oh!"

"Hush, Amelia," said Lucy indignantly. "What difference does that make? He is wounded."

Christian looked up at her searchingly. "I have placed my cards on the table, Miss. What do you think of me now?"

"How delightfully French you sound when you say Mees," Lucy sighed. "I had already guessed you must be the escaped prisoner. My sister thought you to be a poacher, but I could tell from your face that you could not be anything so very cruel. Poachers use traps and bludgeons, you know—the poor animals are tortured before they die when they are caught in a gin trap."

"My escape makes a fracas, yes?" he asked proudly. "You heard of me?"

"Everyone is talking of you," she agreed. "How clever of you to escape! But how did you get wounded? Did they shoot you?"

"That is a long story," he said. "Mon Dieu, but I am thirsty. I could drink a river dry!"

"And we have nothing to give you," she mourned. "We must get you to safety."

Amelia was horrified. She dragged at Lucy's arm, whispering, "We must give him up to the authorities!"

Lucy turned on her. "Would you give up a wounded rabbit to the poacher? You were full of sympathy when you thought an animal was hurt, but because it is only a human being you have lost interest."

"He is French!" Amelia's voice was scandalized.

"He is a fellow being," Lucy retorted. "Only consider! If we give him up, what will become of him? He will be thrust into prison! And in his condition he will most surely die!"

"No," protested Amelia.

"Yes," Lucy insisted. "Even if they put him into the prison hospital his chances must be poor. He might die horribly of blood poisoning or starvation, or gangrene—how often have we heard officers say as much of army hospitals? Suppose that it was Rupert?"

"He would not be ill-treated," Amelia cried. "Rupert has always said that sick prisoners get care!"

"Half the patients die, Amelia," Lucy said scornfully. "Think, would Rachel, however ill we were, send one of us to a public hospital? It would be like signing our death certificate!"

Amelia had to admit the truth of this, and fell

silent before the dreadful picture Lucy painted. It was a public scandal that so many people died in the hospitals. They were foul, neglected cesspits where only the desperate would permit themselves to go.

Lucy bent over their silent companion. "Are you conscious, poor man?"

He looked up at her, a smile curling around his well-cut lips. "I have been listening. You are an angel."

She blushed. "Do you think that if we helped you, you could walk a quarter of a mile to our home?"

"What of your family? Will they not protest? Your Papa?"

"He is dead," Lucy said. "We are orphans, and live with our aunt. She will not turn you from the door, whatever you have done. We have a brother in our own Army. Rachel feels very warmly towards soldiers, for his sake."

"Even French ones?" he asked a little wryly.

"You are superb!" Christian breathed. "What a pity that you are English!"

"I am extremely proud of the fact," she said, insulted.

"Pardon, M'mselle," he said quickly. "I did not mean to be so rude. I meant only that it was tragic that we should find ourselves on opposite sides in this sad conflict."

"War is horrid," she agreed warmly. "For the moment, let us forget about it. We must make shift to move you. Come, try to stand!"

Gently they managed to get him on to his feet. He stood there, breathing heavily, leaning on their shoulders.

The movement, however, had broken open his

wound, which had stiffened while he lay still. He set his teeth grimly and tried to walk. The blood flowed freely, and Lucy groaned.

"We must bind up your wound or you will never manage to get to the cottage!"

While he leaned against a tree, his eyes closed in exhaustion, she tore a strip off the hem of her petticoat, turning her back modestly. They bandaged him as gently as they could, but she saw that his face grew white as death and he shivered as they finished.

Taking off her own cloak she wrapped it around him, ignoring his protests.

"You must keep warm! The worst thing for a man in your condition is to catch cold! Rupert once told me that men die from catching a simple chill because a wound has already lowered their strength."

Somehow they managed to stagger onward through the trees, making slow but steady progress.

When they arrived at the house they pounded on the knocker. A light at last sprang up in an upstairs room. Soon the door opened, and Rachel peered out, holding a candle high to examine them.

"Good God, what is this? Lucy, Amelia, have you been out at such an hour? What has happened? Where have you been? . . ."

"Oh, Rachel," sobbed Amelia, "Let us in. . . . I shall fall down if I do not sit down soon."

Lucy supported Christian alone, her arm about his waist. Now Rachel realized that they had a stranger with them, and her eyes flew wide in horrified astonishment.

"Who is this man, Lucy? Why are you . . ."

Lucy cut her short abruptly. "Rachel, for heaven's sake, do not keep asking questions. We will tell you everything later. For the moment, pray, help us to bring him into the house. . . ."

Rachel stepped back, open-mouthed, and stood her candle upon the small sandalwood chest which stood upon the floor nearby. She and Lucy half dragged Christian into the hall and thence into the little front parlor, where they laid him upon the sofa. He fainted as they released him, his white face falling backwards.

Rachel looked at him in dismay. "Who is he?"

"The French prisoner who escaped," Amelia shrieked, collasping upon a chair. "Oh, Rachel, what shall we do?"

"I am so afraid he will die," Lucy wailed, sinking to her knees beside him and gazing into his face.

Rachel shot a look at her, opened her mouth, then shut it again. She bent over Christian, gently unwinding him from the cloak and examining the blood-stained bandage. "Amelia, run and fetch my scissors from my workbox."

Amelia obeyed, and Rachel cut gently through the bandage, peeling it back to reveal the wound.

Amelia gave a little shriek of horror.

"It is only a flesh wound," Rachel said on a note of satisfaction. "He will not die of it."

"There was so much blood," Lucy protested.

"Naturally," Rachel nodded.

"Was he shot?" Lucy was staring at the wound with firm lips, a determined glint in her eye. Since early childhood she had been convinced that she would make an excellent soldier's wife, and now she had the chance to prove her steel under fire.

"Shot?" Rachel glanced at her, frowning. "No. This is some sort of knife wound, I suspect. You see, it has cut across here, along the ribs. He will have a scar, I am afraid."

Amelia stiffened, staring at the door with fixed eyes. "I heard something," she whispered. "There is someone out there, creeping towards the door!"

They all watched the door tensely. The handle turned. The door slowly creaked open.

Four

Becky's head appeared, her hair fearsomely tied up in a shawl, a pistol wavering in her hand. She stared at them in mute and baffled astonishment.

Rachel smiled at her. "Ah, Becky—just what we needed to put us right! I shall need your advice. Will you put some pans of water on the kitchen fire, and bring me some of that excellent herbal ointment you make?"

"Miss Rachel," Becky said, staring at the wounded man with every appearance of horror. "What is happening here?"

"Becky!" Rachel's voice was firm. "The hot water!"

When Becky had reluctantly departed, Rachel stood up and gave the two girls a penetrating glance. "Now, Miss! Tell me what you have been up to," she said to Lucy.

"Do not blame Amelia," Lucy said frankly. "She was most unwilling to accompany me."

"That I can well believe," Rachel murmured.

"I bullied her into it against her inclination," Lucy said, hanging her head.

"How disgraceful," Rachel observed, watching the white face of the wounded Frenchman with concern. He had not yet recovered consciousness, and she did not like the way he was breathing. It was altogether too shallow and congested. She hoped he had not caught a chill from the night air.

Lucy awaited, realizing that she did not have her aunt's undivided attention.

Rachel turned and looked at her inquiringly. "Well? I am waiting to hear to where you forced Amelia to accompany you?"

"FitzCharles Park," whispered Lucy huskily, her cheeks pink with same.

"Good God!" For the second time, Rachel went white. Her voice grew sharp. "Why should you go there at such an hour?" Her hand clutched at the ribbons of her night gown. "Lucy, what have you been doing?"

"We went to spy upon the ladies," Lucy said in a stammered rush. "That is all—to see their dresses. I so wished to see the newest London fashion. How can one gain a true idea of it from a sketch in a magazine? One must see it worn to get the real impression, and I thought that, as it was a warm night, we might get the chance to look through the windows and catch a glimpse of Mr. FitzCharles's guests in the drawing room."

Rachel's hands slackened, and her tense stance relaxed. "Oh," she sighed. "Thank God. I thought that he . . ." She cut the words off, flushing and looking uneasily at Lucy.

Reassuringly, half indulgently, Lucy said, "You could not think I was so silly as to be lured there, Rachel!"

"After tonight I shall think you silly enough for anything," her aunt said cuttingly.

"I have said that I am sorry," Lucy complained. "And, indeed, Rachel, I shall never do such a thing again. I am punished enough by what occurred."

"What . . . did occur?" Rachel watched her niece like a hawk.

"Why," said Lucy, beginning to enjoy the relating of her tale, "we took the long way through the park because we could not walk up the drive for fear of being seen by the lodgekeeper. We were just approaching the Temple when we saw Mr. FitzCharles."

Rachel stiffened. "Yes?"

"With a female," Lucy breathed.

"Yes," said Rachel dryly. "He would be."

Lucy blinked a little, taken aback by her aunt's expression. Then she went on, "We hid because, of course, we did not wish to be discovered. They were standing a dozen yards or so away, and there was enough light to see them by, but they could not see us because we were in the shadow of the trees."

"I was so frightened," Amelia moaned.

Lucy gave her a disgusted look. "You are so spiritless, Amelia! I was not frightened!"

"Then you should have been," Rachel said, sharply. "What happened?"

Lucy giggled, then went pink. "He . . . he made love to her, and I . . ." she paused, struggling for composure. "I laughed," she burst out.

Amelia rushed into speech at that. "And he heard her, Rachel, and he looked so angry! He came towards us. I was never so terrified in my life! We ran and ran . . . and Lucy lost her locket . . . and we lost our way in the trees and had to go back later because we did not dare to walk along the road for fear of being seen . . . and then, then we heard groans. . . ."

Lucy took up the story. "We found him in a ditch, poor man, and he begged us not to give him up, so we brought him here, not knowing what else to do."

Rachel walked away, and stood, one arm resting on the little mantelpiece above the fire. For a long moment there was silence, then she turned. Her face was pale, and there were shadows under her eyes.

Impulsively Lucy flung her arms around her. "Oh, Rachel, do not, pray, do not look so shocked! I am sorry! Indeed, I am. I know you must feel I have behaved shockingly, and I hate to see you look so grave and sad."

"Do you wonder I look grave?" Rachel looked at her in distress. "What do you think people will say if it ever comes out that you are in the habit of wandering about at night? Once your name is linked with that of . . . of James FitzCharles . . . you will be compromised beyond redemption."

"I told her so," Amelia cried. "She would not listen."

"Then you should have had the courage of your convictions," Rachel said sternly. "It was your place, Amelia, to warn her, not to give in to her folly!"

Amelia burst into tears and rushed from the room.

Lucy sighed. "She is such a goose! She cannot bring herself to oppose me even when she feels I am wrong."

"With your stronger character. Lucy, you should be more in control of your actions. You must learn discretion. Let tonight's events be a lesson to you—we will be fortunate to come out of this scrape without some unhappy consequences." She looked at Lucy's lowered countenance and relented a little. "Well, I shall say no more. We must wait upon the outcome."

Christian moved, at that instant, distracting her

attention. She poured a little wine into a glass and held it to his lips.

"I do not think a little stimulant will do harm," she observed. "Although too much would increase his fever."

She let him sip a few drops, then took the glass away, despite his protest.

"How do you feel?" she asked gently.

"Thirsty," he responded.

She smiled. "You shall have some water in a moment!"

His eyes opened then, and he looked at her wryly. "Water? Must it be water?"

"Be quiet," she reproved gently.

Becky returned at that moment, and the two of them busied themselves with Christian's wound, while Lucy watched, her face steeled against the sick feeling which threatened to overcome her.

"It is by no means as bad as it looks," Rachel said, as she rebandanged. "A flesh wound is always copious of blood. No vital organ is touched."

"Merci," Christian murmured, instinctively, as he lay back against the cushions of the sofa.

Becky stiffened. She gave her mistress a scolding look. "I was never one to mince words, Miss Rachel, so I shall take leave to tell you that you are not acting as you should. Harbor a Frenchie! What would your papa have said?"

Rachel straightened wearily and looked her maid calmly in the face.

"I think he would have said that a human being cannot be regarded solely as the representative of his nation. He also makes demands upon our common humanity."

"Fine words butter no parsnips," Becky snapped. "He's a Frenchie, and our enemy."

"He is a sick man and in need of your excellent nursing Becky," Rachel told her gently.

"What? Me—nurse him?" Becky's voice conveyed her disgust. "I don't know how you can ask it of me, Miss Rachel! He should be handed back to them as knows how to deal with him. Dover Castle—that's where he ought to be!"

"Will you make up the bed in Mr. Rupert's room, Becky?" Rachel returned softly.

Becky's outrage swelled. "Put him in your own nephew's room? You would put him in Master Rupert's room? Well, I'll go to Jericho!"

"Don't do that, Becky," Rachel teased. "We need you here."

"None of your wheedles," Becky said, giving her a fulminating glance. "I know my place, I hope, and I'm not one to question my orders. . . ." She caught Rachel's laughing eye and added tartly. "Don't you make fun of me, Miss. We'll all end in Newgate the way you're going on! They send you to Tower Hill for treason." She drew a hand across her throat. "Yes, that's what they call harboring the King's enemies—high treason!"

Christian struggled to sit upright. "She is in the right," he said stiffly. "I must leave here at once. I do not wish to bring disaster upon such kind people."

Rachel pushed him gently back. "Sir, I am capable of making my own decisions. There is no doing anything about you tonight. The village will be fast asleep. We can make arrangements tomorrow." She smiled at him. "You speak excellent English."

He said wearily, "My mother was English."

"Was?" she probed.

"She died some years ago," he admitted. He looked thirstily at the decanter of wine. Rachel shook her head, but sent Becky to bring him a jug of cold water.

He drank greedily until she took the cup from him for the second time. "That will do, sir. You must not take too much. We must get you upstairs to bed."

"I'll help you," Becky said sturdily.

Rachel smiled at her, her face alight with affection, and the servant grudgingly smiled back.

To distract his mind from the pain his exertions caused him, Rachel asked him as they made their way up the stairs, why he had enlisted as a private soldier in the French army. "You are clearly a gentleman."

"I enlisted without my guardian's permission," he panted. "My parents are both dead. My uncle had other plans for me. I wished to be a soldier, so I ran away and enlisted under a false name. So you see me, the lowest of the low—an infantryman!"

Rachel laughed. "Ah, that is the army talking! It is the same here in England, you know. All the glory is reserved for the cavalry. My brother's friends are very witty upon the subject."

When they had put him to bed, merely removing his boots but none of his other clothes, they left him to sleep and went back downstairs.

Lucy embraced her aunt warmly. "One can always depend upon you to be generous, dearest Rachel!"

"I wish I could depend upon you," Rachel replied tartly.

"I swear I shall reform from tonight," Lucy promised fervently.

"I hope you may," Rachel retorted without conviction.

"You will hide him until he is recovered, won't you?" Lucy then pleaded.

"I am afraid that is not possible, my dear," Rachel said. "Becky is right—it would be too dangerous. He must be handed over to the nearest magistrate tomorrow."

"Rachel, that is Mr. FitzCharles, is it not?" Lucy said, aghast.

Rachel looked astonished. "I believe he is a justice of the peace—but I think it would be best if Ralph dealt with this case."

"Do not give him up!"

"You seem to forget, we are at war," Rachel said.

"Oh, who could forget? With posters on every wall showing Boney the monster; drilling and enlisting going on everywhere, rumors of invasion and spies. I am heartily sick of the war! It has been going on all my life!"

"We are all sick of war, my dear," Rachel agreed. "But we must still do our duty."

"What is our duty?" Lucy cried desperately. "Grandpa always taught us that it is a Christian duty to nurse the sick and comfort the dying!"

"So it is," Rachel agreed. "But sometimes our duties conflict, and then we have a difficult choice to make."

"Well, I think it a great shame," Lucy said, flouncing off to bed.

Rachel sighed, smiled and followed with a weary face.

* * *

Mr. FitzCharles, whatever his custom in London, was used, in the country, to rise early and take a stroll about the park before breakfast.

This habit had been drilled into him in childhood by a father who, because of a sluggish liver brought on in his middle years by an over indulgence at an earlier age, had formed the intention of rearing his sons in healthy habits of living. His eldest son, being the first object of his attentions, had been more strenuously trained in this mode of life, and consequently, the most rebellious in his first years of freedom from parental control.

When the first wild flush of liberty subsided, however, James FitzCharles discovered for himself the lessons his father had tried to drum into his head. An early stroll in the country, he found, gave him an appetite for breakfast, and even more important, cleared the cobwebs of the previous evening's indulgence. Many a hangover had been blown away while he walked briskly through the damp grass, listening to the dawn chorus and beginning to look forward to a plate of ham.

Now, as he came down the private stair which led from his own bedchamber to the stable yard, a convenience first installed by his grandfather, who had spent most of his day in the saddle, he trod softly so as not to disturb the thudding pressure which seemed to center behind his eyes.

Upon returning from his abortive stroll with Lady Danvers, the previous evening, he had rather too freely looked upon the wine while it was red, and was now bitterly regretting it.

Every sound made his veins pound, every movement set up a clash of hammers in the dome of his skull.

Just outside the private door stood a groom in shirtsleeves, his ruddy face cheerful.

"Morning sir!" He led a large hound which leapt at Mr. FitzCharles, whining and snuffling at his hands.

"Gently, Caesar! Manners!" Mr. FitzCharles took the leash from the groom and looked up at the sky. The weather of the previous day persisted, it seemed, but in the east was a scudding row of clouds.

"Going to rain?" He asked the groom.

The man shrugged. "Too early to tell, sir."

As Mr. FitzCharles turned away, the groom exclaimed, "Oh, by the way, sir, when Prickitt was coming through the park this morning he found an object."

What manner of object?" Mr. FitzCharles asked with amusement.

The groom dived into the nearest loose box and came out with a tattered garment. "This, sir. He found it in the west covert, sir, near the dry ditch."

Mr. FitzCharles turned it over. "Interesting."

"A French uniform, sir?" suggested the groom.

His master gave him a reflective glance. "The escaped prisoner, Miller?"

The groom lifted his shoulders in an acquiescent shrug. That's obvious, his gesture said in some surprise. Aloud, he asked, "Shall I get the men together and search again, sir?"

Mr. FitzCharles hesitated still. Then he nodded. "Yes, but take care not to say anything to my guests. I do not wish to alarm the ladies." He gazed across the stable yard, his lean features a cold mask. "If you do find him, Miller, lock him into the bailiff's office and mount a guard upon him until I see him." He paused. "I want it understood that no one is to talk to this man until I have seen him. No violence, Miller." He shot him a glance. "Do you comprehend me? Just march the fellow back here and send for me."

Miller nodded. He looked a little affronted. "I'm sure we would not lay a finger on him, sir," he said stiffly. He pointed to a dark stain. "Had you noticed this, sir?"

Mr. FitzCharles touched the jacket with one long finger. "Blood?" he mused aloud.

"Might be an old stain, of course, sir," Miller said.

"It looks very new to me, but you may be right. Carry on, Miller. I will take Caesar for his stroll."

Miller looked at him dubiously. "In the park, sir?"

"You fancy he may attack me? Do you know, I doubt that, Miller," drawled Mr. FitzCharles. He looked down at the dog. "Well, Caesar, what do you think?"

The hound dropped his fine-boned head into his master's outstretched hand and gazed at him with melancholy eyes. He was very tired of all this talking and wished to be off investigating the various interesting odors which assailed him from all quarters.

"Exactly my own view," smiled Mr. FitzCharles, pinching the dog's chin gently. "Come, we will take our walk. I suppose that will please you, you importunate hound?"

Caesar raised his head and barked loudly, then set off at a gallop, his long legs skidding on the grass, his tail beating. A pheasant whirred up from some long grass and vanished into the trees. Caesar rocketed after him.

"Heel," shouted his master, and, as the dog returned, said sternly, "Yes, you know better than that, sir. I see you have been grossly overindulged during my absence. I fancy you need a strong hand. You appear lost to all sense of decency. I wonder, now, are you allowed always to run wild in the park, scaring my game to shreds, while I am in London? I wonder my keepers permit it. I must look into the matter."

The dog sighed heavily, and he said to it with amusement, "Oh, yes, you are penitent, I dare say, but you must relearn old habits, my friend, if you are not to end up as a crow-scarer."

Caesar nuzzled his hand, the liquid eyes melting. "Fawning wretch," said Mr. FitzCharles with amusement. "You do not need a tongue, with those great eyes of yours. . . ."

They then proceeded at a staider pace until, lured by the sudden blur of a white's rabbit's tail, Caesar fell from grace once more and set off in pursuit, deaf to all his master's whistling; scrabbling and barking through the ferny undergrowth, sending up showers of leaf and twigs in his wake.

"Come out of there at once sir," snapped Mr. FitzCharles. "Bad dog! Do you understand me? Bad!" Caesar, his paws and jaw muddy, a piece of leaf absurdly protruding from his lower lip, barked joyfully, wagging his tail.

"I gave up all hope of you," sighed his master. "You are an incorrigible rascal."

He straightened and turned, halting in midstride as he found himself staring through the trees at a white blur. Caesar waited impatiently, wondering what was wrong now.

Below them rose the chimneys of the White House, in which the Duncans lived. Mr. FitzCharles put his hand into his waistcoat pocket and brought out something that glittered. He half-moved forward, smiling oddly to himself, then thurst the little object back into his pocket and walked rapidly back to the house, followed by a very puzzled dog.

He was amazed to find, when he entered the breakfast room, that his Mama was seated at the table with a pot of hot chocolate before her.

Kissing her lightly he asked, "Why, what does this mean, Mama? Are you reformed? I have not known you rise before noon this ten years past!"

"Nonsense!" She shook her head at him. "I get up when I have cause, dear boy."

"And what is this cause which prompts so drastic a change in your habits today?" His teasing tone was accompanied by an affectionate smile which took away any sting she might have suspected.

"I am going to pay a morning call," she said. "I have asked for the carriage to be brought round in half an hour."

He sat down and looked at her intently. "A morning call," he repeated slowly. "On whom, Mama?"

She sipped her chocolate. "On Rachel Duncan, my dear."

There then followed a silence. After a while he drew a harsh breath. "No, Mama!"

She widened her eyes. "James, I have known Rachel this twenty seven years—I remember when she was born. . . ."

"Twenty six," he automatically corrected.

She smiled at him. "Why, so she is! I can hardly believe it. And you are thirty!"

He moved restlessly. "For God's sake, Mama. . . ." His words were bitten off. He was silent again for a moment, then said, "I would prefer it if you did not go, Mama."

"Why?" she asked point-blank.

"She would not expect it. She knows you rarely go out. You have not paid calls for years. Why begin now?"

"I wish to see here," she answered firmly. "I was always very fond of her and I have been wishing to see her again for a long time."

He took some thick slices of pink ham from a silver dish and laid them upon his plate. She watched him begin to eat. After a while he said, "You are determined?"

"Determined," she said softly.

He shrugged. "I see, Mama, but I tell you frankly, if your reasons are what I suspect them to be, you will be wasting your time."

"Have you spoken to Bailey since you arrived?" she asked.

He looked surprised. "I am not so eager to be closeted with my bailiff that I haste to see him the second I arrive, Mama. I shall be seeing him very soon, no doubt. Bailey always insists on such lengthy interviews and gives me such a wealth of detail about the estate that I need to be in the best of health before I send for him."

"He tells me she is on the point of becoming engaged to Ralph Mellows," Mrs. FitzCharles murmured casually.

His hand halted halfway to his lips. She watched with her penetrating blue stare. At last he gave a short laugh. "Does he, indeed? Pray, wish her happy when you see her!" He chewed a little more ham, then pushed the plate away, saying irritably, "I should not have taken so much wine last night. I have a head like a furnace this morning."

"Poor James," she said gently.

Five

When the carriage halted outside the White House Rachel was in the front garden, filling a rush basket with the petals which had dropped from her roses overnight. Dried in the sun and added to a judicious mixture of other dried flowers, they would stand around her rooms in delicate porcelain bowls for months, perfuming the air with memories of summer.

Hearing the grating wheels, she turned and gave the carriage a startled apprehensive look which altered as she saw the groom help Mrs. FitzCharles down.

She ran to greet her. "Why, Ma'am—this is an unexpected honor. I had not looked to see you here. I had thought your health would deny me that pleasure, but it is delightful to see you again at last."

"Rachel," said Mrs. FitzCharles, taking her hands and gazing at her affectionately. "Is it two years?"

"Nearer three," admitted Rachel. "Come into the parlor and have a glass of Becky's elderflower wine." She caught the older woman's expression and laughed. "We do not keep a cellar now, you know, for it was only for Papa that we stocked anything stronger than home-brewed. Now and then someone presents us with a bottle of brandy, of course."

Mrs. FitzCharles looked at her with eyes that twinkled. "Of course," she agreed smoothly. They both laughed. In the Kent countryside the generous donors of these bottles of brandy were never named. Free trading was a creed unchallenged by local gentry.

Even Mrs. FitzCharles, who lived largely in London now, knew the origin of such gifts and took them for granted.

In the house, Mrs. FitzCharles looked around the parlor with a nostalgic sigh. "How familiar it all seems. I could expect your dear Papa to come through that door at any moment and read me a sermon on going to sleep during service, as I invariably did. I am afraid I found the air in church so stifling in summer, and we were usually here in summer. Is the new man satisfactory? I have hardly seen him since he was appointed, although I do remember him when he was curate here."

"He is a good creature, but very much under his wife's thumb," said Rachel, smiling.

"Ah, it is like that, is it?" Mrs. FitzCharles smiled. "And you, my dear, how do you go on? You do not seem much changed."

Rachel's glance was gently ironic. "I am three years older, Ma'am, and it shows."

"Only if one looks closely," the other woman said. "It is in the eyes that I see a change. You have lost something of your old gaiety, and I am sorry to see it." She paused. "I hear news of you from Bailey that surprises me. Can it be true that you are about to accept Ralph Mellows?"

Rachel's chin lifted. "If it were true, why should it surprise you? He is of good family and excellent reputation. He will offer me a pleasant home and make an attentive, affectionate husband. Why should I not accept him?"

"Do not fly up into the air, my love," soothed Mrs. FitzCharles. "I have no doubt Ralph is all you say, yet I could not be glad to see you marry him."

Their eyes met. Rachel's fell, her color deepening in her averted face.

Idly Mrs. FitzCharles murmured. "James wished to accompany me this moning, but I wished to have your undivided attention."

"I am very sure he will find more pleasant diversions with his guests," Rachel said sharply.

"James is not happy. He is restless and difficult. I would like to see him settled. The diversions you refer to are mere childish defiance, my love. He was always the same, even as a small boy—when he wished for attention he would do something naughty, preferring even punishment to being ignored."

Rachel moved away restlessly. "Another glass of elderflower wine?"

Mrs. FitzCharles looked at her regretfully. "My dear, I have never begged anyone for anything in my life before. You must be well aware how much I would wish to see a certain event, how dearly I would welcome you. . . ."

Rachel rose, flushing. "Pray, Mrs. FitzCharles, say no more. . . . I do not think this is a matter on which we could ever come to agree, and it wounds me to . . ." She broke off as the door flew open and Lucy rushed into the room.

"Oh, Rachel, do pray come at once . . . he is quite feverish. I do not know what to do!" She faltered to a stop as she saw the other woman in the room. "Oh, good morning, Mrs. FitzCharles; I did not know you were here."

"How are you, Lucy?" replied Mrs. FitzCharles

with a sigh. She had hoped to have Rachel to herself for much longer, and felt great disappointment. She had only just touched upon her true mission here this morning, and did not wish to be deflected before she had made a serious attempt to persuade Rachel to listen to her.

Rachel, however said, "I must apologise, Mrs. FitzCharles, but we have an invalid on our hands, and I am afraid I must leave you to attend to him. Lucy will fetch you some tea, if you wish, and sit and talk with you."

Mrs. FitzCharles bowed to the inevitable. She saw, from Rachel's tone, and her expression, that she had, as James had predicted, been wasting her time.

"No," she said sadly. "I will not detain Lucy, thank you, my love. I must go. I hope the invalid is not dear Rupert?"

Lucy looked at her sister with agitation. Rachel calmly shook her head. "It is a friend of the family, Ma'am. Rupert, so far as we know, is in the best of health, and enjoying the military life as much as ever. I am sorry that your visit has been interrupted in this fashion. It was kind of you to call. I am very glad to have seen you once again, indeed."

"Are you, my dear?" the older woman asked her wistfully.

Rachel softened, and gave her an impulsive hug. "Indeed, you know I am! I have always been most sincerely attached to you."

She came to the door of the carriage to see Mrs. FitzCharles safely bestowed inside, and waved her on her way.

Turning back, she saw a tall figure step out from the concealing shelter of an elm tree further along the lane, and her heart thrust fiercely against her side.

While she halted in surprise he crossed the lane slowly and looked at her, his dark face intent.

"You do not change," he said, in a very deep voice.

Rachel felt anger sweep up inside her. "Your mother told me you had not come with her," she said, half in accusation.

"I followed on foot. She was unaware of my presence." His face changed, the disturbing intensity leaving it. Lightly, he said, "I wished to see your niece."

Her eyes widened, lifting to his face in bewilderment. "My niece?"

He drew the locket from his waistcoat and dangled it in front of her. "She lost it last night."

She looked at it, then at him. "Yes," she said, in biting contempt. "She told me of her escapade."

For a flashing second she saw a confusion of emotions in his eyes—regret, shame, self-irritation. Then his lip curled in derision. "I trust she did not give any details?"

Her cold glance withered him. "I fancy she did, sir."

He smiled mockingly. "Her education was advanced last night, I imagine."

She half turned away, her face white with anger. "How can you laugh on such a topic! It is intolerable. . . ."

He moved, briefly, as if about to touch her arm, then drew back again, laughing. "Why the provincial mind does not change, I see, my dear!"

She reached abruptly for the locket. He snatched it out of reach.

"Oh, no," he mocked. "I prefer to give it to the young lady herself!"

"I am afraid that will be impossible," she retorted. "Lucy is very busy."

He glanced past her at the open door of the house. "So I see," he drawled lazily.

She swung round and found Lucy hovering there, half impatient for her to come in to look at Christian, half-horrified by the appearance of Mr. FitzCharles upon their doorstep.

He walked up the path before Rachel had notice of his intention, and Lucy shrank back against the door, blushing violently and looking away.

He lounged in front of her, smiling, his glance moving over her with amused curiosity.

"I have a pretty thing," he murmured. "And a very pretty thing . . . I wonder whose pretty thing this may be. . . ." The words of the old nursery rhyme sounded taunting and improvised upon his lips as he held up the locket.

Lucy put out a hand at once, but he would not release the locket. His fingers merely caught hers and held them tightly. "Do you know the game of forfeits? What will you give me in return for this locket, Lucy? A kiss?"

"That is enough, sir!" Rachel's voice snapped like a whip. She stepped between her niece and Mr. FitzCharles, giving him an angry, scornful glance. "Lucy, go to your room. Sir, give me the locket."

Lucy whirled into the house, her skirts flouncing around her feet.

Mr. FitzCharles gazed at Rachel. "Do I get no forfeit?" he asked, still smiling, yet with a curious twist to his mouth. "I will accept a proxy."

Their eyes met. Her color rose at the challenge in

his. "You are behaving abominably," she told him curtly.

"What did you call me that day . . . a rake . . . a gamester . . . what else was it?" His tone was light, but beneath it ran a darker thread.

"A fool," she said tightly.

"So I am," he agreed. "The biggest in the world."

"I had not thought you would stoop to blackmail, though," she said cuttingly.

His face paled. "I use what weapons I have," he said with sudden savagery. "They are few enough, God knows. Would you have me utterly defenseless?"

Without a word she held out her hand for the locket, her expression cold.

With a wry smile he capitulated, dropping it into her palm, then, before she could drag it way, seized her hand and kissed the palm with a brief, passionate gesture.

They stood, like wrestlers searching for an advantage, then she pulled her hand back, stepped into the house and shut the door in his face.

Lucy was hovering on the stairs, her face bewildered. "Did you get the locket?"

Rachel, white to the lips, silently held out her hand, revealing the locket on her palm. Lucy took it, her eyes uncertainly trying to probe the defenses her aunt put up to hide her thoughts. "Will you come and see Christian now?"

"In a moment," Rachel said huskily. "Go up. I will follow you shortly."

Lucy hesitated, then obeyed. Rachel leaned against the wall, shivering as if she had an ague. Her eyes closed tightly, she wrapped her arms around herself, rocking to and fro, breathing raggedly. Then, straightening with a deep sigh, she composed her features to follow Lucy up the stairs.

Lucy was waiting for her on the landing outside Christian's room. "Oh, I am sure he is going to die," Lucy whispered. "He looks so ill! When I put my hand upon his forehead I quite shuddered to feel how hot it was."

"Clear your mind of such anxiety," Rachel soothed. "The wound was by no means a fatal one. I will look at him. I am certain I will find him merely a trifle feverish, as is to be expected after losing so much blood."

When she stood beside the bed and looked down at Christian, tossing on his pillows, she lost her confident air, however, and grew grave.

"I am very much afraid you may be right," she said soberly. "He does not, indeed, look as he ought. I think I must send for Mr. Foulkes. I should not care to neglect any opportunity to save the poor young man."

Lucy looked dismayed. "If you send for Mr. Foulkes we will have to let the authorities take Christian away!"

"My dear, we must do so in any case. There can be now no question of moving him from this bed, though—he is clearly far too ill. The exposure and lack of nursing must have been more of a shock to his system than I had anticipated. With such a strong, healthy young man I had been more hopeful than wise. I thought he would soon throw off the evil effects of his wound, but I see I was wrong."

Christian was tossing more and more restlessly, his handsome face flushed, his skin bearing the high glaze which so disturbed her, his eyes half-shut, his lids flickering constantly, as though he dreamt unpleasantly.

Lucy laid her hand upon his forehead. "Oh, he is so hot," she whispered in a tone of great anxiety.

"The fever has taken strong hold," agreed Rachel.

"Do you think he will be bled?"

"He has already lost too much blood," Rachel said firmly.

"When old Gammy Lammeter was gored by the bull at Lime Farm he was bled," Lucy reminded her.

"And died of it!" Rachel retorted.

They both turned as Becky entered the room. "Oh, Becky," Rachel said with relief. "I am so glad you are here. Will you look at this boy—he has gone into a high fever. Should we send for Mr. Foulkes, would you say? Your opinion must be heard for you have more experience of illness than any of us!"

Becky bent over the bed for a few moments, then said tartly, 'What can that old butcher do here? You did not expect the boy to go scot free, did you, after lying on damp grass at night, which is worse than anything, as I have told you children time and time again. I have made him a nice tisane of camomile to cool his blood. You let him be for a while. Leave me to do the nursing, and just get on with making that blackcurrant jelly you promised me. Time is all that is needed here."

Rachel smiled at her lovingly. "A tower of strength, Becky! What would we do without you? Come, Lucy, we will go down to the kitchen and set about making this jelly, for it is Becky's favorite, you know, and if she is to nurse Frenchmen, she deserves a reward."

Becky looked at her grimly. "Don't you come awheedling me, Miss!"

Rachel was not fooled by her brisk tone. She kissed her cheek and gave her a hug before whisking Lucy away.

"Rachel, do not give him up yet," Lucy begged, as they went downstairs. "If the army come and take him away he might die."

Rachel looked uncertainly at her. "Ralph will visit us in the next day or so, I belive, and I shall wait until he comes here before informing anyone of Christian's presence."

Lucy gave her a sideways look, her eyes gleaming with curiosity. She had been much struck by that odd little scene between her aunt and Mr. FitzCharles. There had been an unreal quality about Mr. FitzCharles's teasing, as if he was not really aware of her at all, although he had pretended to kiss her. Her fear when she saw that he had her locket and knew of her presence in his park on the previous evening had evaporated as she came to realize that he was quite indifferent to the scandalous nature of her own behavior, but was using it, in some way she did not comprehend, for his own ends. When he spoke to her aunt there had been a quite noticeable difference in his face and voice which had puzzled her, and which now came back to her.

"Did you inform Mr. FitzCharles that you had the French prisoner upstairs?" she asked a little shyly.

To her surprise her aunt blushed. "No," she said curtly.

Lucy opened her eyes wide. "Why not?"

"I forgot," Rachel snapped.

Lucy looked at her again, with a fresh interest, seeing her aunt as she had never seen her before; noting the beauty with which she was so familiar that she never took account of it, the dark hair, calm oval face and fine features.

"You must have been pretty when you were my age, Rachel," she said, pityingly, and wondered why her aunt burst out laughing.

Six

As luncheon drew to a close at FitzCharles Park that day Sir Henry Danvers leaned forward and said gruffly to his host, "I saw your men out in the park with dogs. After the escaped prisoner, were they? They seemed to be reluctant to answer questions on the matter."

Reaching one long hand for an apricot from the bowl in the center of the table, Mr. FitzCharles smiled blandly. "They were searching for the Frenchman, yes."

"Sound notion!" enthused Freddy. "Why didn't you let me get out with them, James? I call that selfish of you. Did they find, eh?"

"Unfortunately, no," his brother drawled. "The dogs seemed to pick up the scent at one stage, but then they ran out of the Park and seemed set on running through every house in the village, so the hunt had to be given up. Half the women in the village were by then in hysterics."

His secretary, a slim colorless young man, who dined with the family owing to a distant kinship with his employer, remarked that he rather supposed the Frenchman was halfway across the channel by now. "He would be a fool to remain in this neighborhood. I doubt if he ever was anywhere near the Park in the first place."

Mr. FitzCharles gave him a smile. "Quite so,"

he murmured. "But on the other hand, there was that confounded jacket."

Freddy dropped a knife with a clatter, and leaned forward with bursting excitement. "What's that? Have you been holding out on us, James? What an oyster you are!"

Mr. FitzCharles grinned carelessly at him. "I did not wish to burden my men with a parcel of amateur beaters like you, Freddy! Had the fellow been armed, consider my dismay had he shot you! Inconsolable, I assure you, dear brother!"

Freddy grimaced threateningly. "No such thing, you hypocrite!"

"Oh, I protest," Mr. FitzCharles murmured. "I should, after all, have had to wear mourning for an intolerable period."

Freddy hooted with laughter. "Come, brother, unburden yourself, or I swear I will cut your throat with your own fruit knife!"

Mr. FitzCharles graphically described the discovery of the bloodstained jacket, bringing a shriek from Isabella, and a whoop of glee from Freddy. "Why, he must have been in the park all the time, and those clods from the village walked right by him and never even knew it!"

"Undoubtedly," agreed his brother. He glanced at his secretary. "And while I think of it, Brown, it might be as well if you conveyed this information to the Constable of Dover Castle. They will be interested to hear that evidence has been found to suggest that he did in fact hide in the Park. If they wish to do so, pray inform them that they may send some soldiers to make a further search for him."

"Since he has undoubtedly now left it would seem

a pointless waste of time," Brown said. "But I will write as you suggest, sir."

He then excused himself and left the room, Freddy stared after him with dislike.

"Damned clerk! Gives me the shivers. Always was a smooth-tongued, secretive fellow!"

His brother shook his head at him reprovingly. "I depend upon him, Freddy. He is very efficient."

Sir Henry said loudly. "Excellent thing, efficiency. Too much of the opposite in this country—inefficiency at the top, runs right down through the whole nation. War cabinet—set of buffoons!"

"Oh, quite," murmured Mr. FitzCharles, hastily passing the decanter.

His mother gave him a cross look and rose. "We will withdraw," she said in a tone of great dignity. "James, I wish to speak to you in the library in half an hour."

He bowed. "Certainly, Mama."

When the door had closed behind the ladies Sir Henry recklessly poured himself a brimming glass and drained it with a belligerent air. "I believe information leaks from the war cabinet faster than from an old bucket. I wouldn't give them charge of my stables let alone this country! England's doomed. We'll have that fellow, that Corsican upstart, over here before you can say knife. Sitting on His Majesty's throne, I should not wonder—obviously after a crown."

"Oh, do you think so?" Mr. FitzCharles asked, since it was clearly expected of him to say something.

Sir Henry glared at him. "As soon as this wedding's over I shall go back to my estates. Organize! Get my people on a real war footing. None of this half and half stuff—that's just playing at it. The French know how to do things. Every able-bodied man who can be spared straight into the services. That's how to win!"

"You are too pessimistic, Sir Henry," drawled Mr. FitzCharles. "Certainly we have our share of fools in office, but they are honest fools, you know, and they are Englishmen. If Bonaparte set foot on English soil, which God forbid, he would find a warm welcome, not one he would enjoy. You have not toured the coastal areas, as I have, and seen the spirit of the people. They can be obstinate, wilful, even downright rascals—but they are ready for him, should he come, and it is those very qualities which irritate us in peace time which will win the war for us tomorrow."

"D'you think he will invade, James?" Freddy asked.

"I doubt it. He knows the task is beyond him. He will soon be ready to come to terms."

"That is not what I hear," said Freddy.

Sir Henry snorted. "No, he makes ludicrous demands in return for a treaty, such demands as could only add up to total surrender on our part. I hear, too, that the government is running about like a chicken with its head cut off trying to find ways of giving in to him on every point. If they should do so, if such a humiliating treaty should be signed, I make no bones about it, sir, I for one would never accept it! No self-respecting Englishman could!"

Mr. FitzCharles picked up his glass and frowned at the wine, twirling the twisted stem between his long fingers so that the light danced over the surface of the red wine. "I do not know where you got this information, sir, but I assure you, the source is tainted. The first negotiations in matters like these are always mere opening moves. Pure bluff on both sides. There's no danger of any paper being signed which would be unacceptable to the country at large."

Sir Henry gave a snort. "My friends say otherwise!"

He received a cool glance. "I fear you are unwise to listen to them. They are not always clear-headed."

Sir Henry reddened. "How dare you, sir!"

"You really should take with a pinch of salt what comes from the headquarters of the opposition," sighed Mr. FitzCharles. "The treaty is an official secret—the fact that negotiations are in fact proceeding is not for general publication. Your friends should not be so loose in the tongue. It is always a delicate business finding common ground with an enemy. The less said in public during such negotiations the better."

Freddy stammered, "B-b-but dammit, James, I've known this age that a treaty was afoot. Who has not? Every wit in the coffee houses knows of it."

Sir Henry's back was stiff, his eye affronted. "Are you accusing me of indiscretion, sir?" he demanded, ready to call his host to account in a trice.

He was given a smile. "Sir, we as well as the French need a breathing space in which to recoup. I do not imagine, any more than yourself, that we are done with the Corsican, even if we do eventually sign a treaty with him. He is too ambitious, and the fanatics he leads are too convinced of their duty to teach the world the path of revolution. But, I repeat, if this treaty gives us a much-needed opportunity to strengthen our arm, it will be extremely useful.

At the moment each of us is uncertain how far the other is prepared to give way. I am sure you would not wish to put into peril the whole of our diplomatic strategy by giving the Frenchmen a false idea of our nation's strength."

Sir Henry rose. "I detest diplomacy," he said sturdily. "It is of all things the most pernicious practice. I cannot be doing with all these lies and counter-lies. I like things plain and simple. Then I know where I am."

"I respect your attitude, but I fear it would not do in international circles. There is a pattern laid down which has been tested over the years. Diplomacy is a matter of tact and discretion. Now, if you will excuse me, I must join my Mama in the library. You will wish to sit with the ladies in the drawing room, I've no doubt. I will see you there in a little while."

When he entered the library he was smiling, and his mother turned to greet him with a glance of curiosity. "What is amusing you now, James?"

He gave her the gist of the conversation which had occurred after she had left the dining room, and she laughed. "Poor Sir Henry, alas, he would be lost in the maze of the diplomatic minuet!"

"A very mixed metaphor, Mama," he teased. "Now, what is this important subject you wished to discuss with me?"

She folded her hands in her lap, looking at him soberly. "James, you went to the White House this morning, despite my warning to you."

A flush rose in his face. "How the devil do you find out these things?" he burst out.

"I saw you as I drove away," she said.

He turned away and sauntered to the bookshelves, fingering the spines of the books in an absent way. "Well, what of it?" he said defiantly.

"How foolish of you, James!"

"I am aware of it, Mama."

"Then why did you do it?"

"I could not help myself. I had not seen her for so long. The temptation was irresistible."

"For a man who plays the diplomatic game with so much skill and insight, if I am to believe your superiors, you are a remarkably poor tactician when it comes to affairs of the heart!"

"You know me too well, Mama. It is disconcerting to be so transparent." He walked across the room towards her, his expression grim. "I made a fool of myself this morning. I tried to make her jealous by flirting with that silly little niece of hers, and only succeeded in damning myself further."

"James, James," she sighed, "What am I to do with you? Are you quite blind to Rachel's character? Brought up by that excellent but unbending old man, her father, she could never be expected to accept your folly. Her principles are too rigidly instilled."

"She seems so gentle, so sweet of temper," he flung wildly. "Why is she never so to me?"

"My poor blind boy, Rachel is all you have said, but her sweetness and gentleness are never an excuse for weakness. She dislikes your way of life, she disapproves of your worldly amusements."

"When she refused me three years ago I determined to put the whole episode behind me, as you know. I wish to God it had been possible." He struck his forehead with a clenched fist. "Why did I have to fall irretrievably in love with a parson's daughter?"

"If you could only be a little less ham-minded, James," his mother chided him. "Flirting with other females is not the way to convince any woman that you are sincere in your protest of love for herself!"

"I know that," he snapped. "When I am with her I seem to lose my common sense. The truth is, Mama, I cannot bear to have her look at me with such dislike. I feel such rage, such pain, that I can only try to inflict the same in return, by wild fits of folly like this. . . ."

"You have played your cards all wrong from the very start," said Mrs. FitzCharles sadly. "When you came back home after your father's death and fell in love with Rachel I knew it would not be easy for you to win her. Did it never occur to you that your exploits in London would have been noised abroad down here? Everyone knew of the dancer you kept, even the color of the carriage you had bought her!"

"Mama," he interrupted. "Spare my blushes, I beg you. . . ."

"Be quiet, James! There were so many silly incidents! That ludicrous duel you fought with Alexander Tolcarrow over the Smirton chit—it was not three days later that I heard every detail from my own maid!"

"What gossips you all are, Mama!"

"It is the way of the world, my son, and villages are worse than anything. With your reputation, to take one glance at Rachel and commence a pursuit of her so blatant as to be insulting . . ."

"I wished to marry her!" He was stung into rage.

"Maybe so, but you were too hot too soon. She could not take seriously such an onslaught. She thought, I suspect, that you planned seduction, knowing the great difference in your stations, and your careful avoidance of matrimony until that time."

"But when I proposed!"

"She took it to be evidence of your spoilt desire to have your own way, I think. Rachel has a strong character. She would not lightly give her heart, nor would she put up with the sort of behavior she thought she might expect from you once the gloss of marriage wore off. She presumably believed that you might come to resent having made such a match, and would return to your old pursuits."

"Return to other women when I had her? I would never be tempted, Mama. I know that."

"I am convinced of it," she agreed gently. "I have observed that although you have made a great deal of noise about your pleasures these past years you have in reality been working very hard at your career, and it has been more a case of much smoke, very little fire."

He laughed reluctantly. "Shrewd, Mama. And true. I take little pleasure in such amusements now."

"Then why, oh why, my son, did you pretend to do so? Why give Rachel every reason to believe her assessment of you a just one? Why did you not patiently lay siege to her? You have had three years in which to build up trust and reliance in her, but you rushed back to London and plunged into every sort of wild activity, deliberately designed, I believe, to underline her doubts of you."

"I was out of my mind with disappointment," he admitted. "I did not care what I did so long as I contrived to show her how little I cared for her rejection."

"How could you make so foolish a mistake?"

He laughed. "I adore you, Mama, when you put on that fierce face—you look like a cross kitten!"

"James, will you be serious?" she implored him.

His face altered and he looked at her very soberly indeed.

"Very well," she nodded. "I will help you. Will you follow my advice?"

"Absolutely," he nodded.

"You will sever all connections with Lady Danvers, for a beginning. I know it was never more than a game, but the game must stop. Then you will begin to court Rachel with patience and quietness. You will flirt with no one, you will not game or be seen at wild parties. You will become a new man."

"I am to be a reformed character, am I?" He gave a twisted smile. "It will go against the grain, Mama. I am used to a very different life."

"James, do you think I have not noticed lately how you have sickened of London? You keep a mask on your face for your friends, but I have known you since babyhood. I have seen the mask slip when you thought yourself unobserved. You have long been wishing to settle here at the Park, have you not?"

He sighed. "Shrewd and observant Mama, yes. Yes, I have. I find an odd tug pulling at my heart when I think of this place. I would like sons to grow up here, as I did, and time to feel myself part of a family again."

"Rachel is a country girl, she likes the quiet country ways and is not made to lead a town life. That may have influenced her when she refused you. She has never shown any fancy for London. Take my advice, my boy, do not rush in upon her, proclaiming yourself a reformed man. Let her realize you mean to stay here. Let her grow used to seeing you about the place. Sometimes, James, it is wise to withhold yourself. Can you be patient?"

He took her hand and formally kissed the back. "I will try. I cannot promise, but I will try."

Lucy sat beside Christian's bed, gently smoothing down the sheets over his restless, moving hands. Her admiring gaze wandered over his handsome face and tumbled dark hair. She sighed. He was the hero she had dreamed about all her life—brave, daring, handsome—and in danger! His birth made him altogether perfect because it made their love as remote as a fairy tale, an impossible, unattainable star.

He twisted uneasily on the pillow and she bent forward, catching a mumbled phrase.

"Must see him . . . FitzCharles . . . must see him . . . help. . . ."

She frowned. The words trailed off in an incoherent jumble. He moved his head, moistening his dry lips. She saw the perspiration gleaming on his forehead.

Quietly, she rose and went to the table behind her, on which lay a bowl of cool water, a sponge, a jug and a cup.

She picked up the sponge and dipped it in the water, squeezed gently, then went back to sponge his forehead.

At the first touch of the wet sponge he jerked his head almost off the pillow, shouting, "FitzCharles—no!" His voice was so tense that she froze on the spot, her eyes wide with shocked incredulity.

His eyes flew open. He stared at her blankly for

a second, then with dawning recognition. "M'mselle . . . so I did not dream you! You are real!"

"Of course I am real," she said, smiling delightedly back. "I was just going to cool your face with the sponge. You are so hot. It will make you feel better."

"You are very kind," he said, settling back contentedly, his lips curving in a smile.

Gently she wiped his face. "There! Is that not better?"

"Much better," he agreed. "Thank you."

She brought him a cup of water, and he drank greedily. "Ah," he sighed. "That was good! I cannot remember ever tasting anything so delicious! How can I thank you?"

"You have already done so often," she laughed. "It is nothing, I assure you!"

"Nothing?" He looked at her passionately. "How can you say so? I am allowing you to risk your lives by sheltering me!"

She blushed and shook her head in disagreement.

"I see I embarrass you," Christian said quickly. "I understand your delicacy and modesty. I will say no more, but please believe that I feel more than I could ever say!" He took her hand and raised it to his lips.

Lucy looked at him through lowered lashes. Her heart was beating as fast as a drum. This was much more exciting than any of the dreams she had entertained in the weary hours before he came into her life. Sometimes she almost felt that she must awake, and find that, after all, she had dreamt this, too.

There was an uncomfortable little silence, then, to fill in the gap between them, Lucy asked brightly,

"Why do you keep talking about Mr. FitzCharles? Can it be possible that you know him?"

He froze, staring at her. "Quoi?" He was startled into speaking his native tongue, then, at her baffled expression, went on, "What do you mean?"

"In your sleep you talked of him," she said.

"I must not tell you," he said unhappily. "It might endanger your life!"

Seeing that here was a mystery, Lucy became determined to find it out. Christian could not know, but he had chosen the worst possible approach. Now she would never be content until she knew what lay behind his gnomic utterance. Using all her coaxing ways, her pouts and smiles, she nagged at him for a further hour before she managed to persuade him to tell her the whole story.

"But, I implore you, swear not to tell anyone what I shall confide to you," Christian begged her first.

"Oh, I do," she assured him eagerly. "I swear it!"

"Very well," he nodded. "Then—Mr. FitzCharles is an agent of my country's secret police."

"An agent of . . ." she repeated, bewildered. Then her eyes grew round with horror. "Oh! You mean he is a spy! A French spy!" She flushed scarlet then grew white. "Good heavens, I cannot believe it! Why would Mr. FitzCharles spy for France?"

"I imagine—for money," he shrugged. "Or perhaps because he believes in the revolutionary cause. There are many such in England. My uncle is in charge of that part of the secret police, and they encourage such sympathizers with money to organize themselves. . . ."

"You mean . . . Radicals?" she cried in dismay.

"That is what you call them, I believe. There are

many societies in England which exist to further the revolutionary cause."

She looked at him shyly. "Christian . . . are you a revolutionary?"

His dark face glowed. "It is a noble ideal! Why should one man be superior to another? Did God make him so? No, it was mere accident of birth."

"You told us that you were a gentleman," she said, instinctively putting a finger on the weakness of his beliefs.

He flushed, then grimaced. "Ah, like all women you go to the weak spot in a man! I was born a gentleman, yes, and I suppose I cannot escape the instincts of heredity. My education taught me the wisdom of the people. . . ."

"They murdered their King," she said impulsively.

He sighed. "Your King is a good man, perhaps. Our King was not—he cared less for his people than for his dogs."

"I do not understand politics," she said thoughtfully. "But it seems to me that murder can never be a way of righting wrongs." She shrugged. "But do not let us fall out over it. Tell me—why do you suspect Mr. FitzCharles of being a spy?"

"I know he is a spy," Christian said. "I met him in France. My uncle sent me to see him once. I had almost forgotten him, but when we were on our way to Dover the coach went past and I saw a face I remembered very well—the English spy whom my uncle found so useful. I escaped and went to find him."

"Did you find him?" she gasped.

"I did, and he tired to kill me," he said bitterly.

"He stabbed me—I should have known better than to trust a proven traitor."

"Oh, shocking," she whispered. "Mr. FitzCharles . . . much as I dislike him I cannot believe it . . ."

Christian looked insulted. "I would not lie to you!"

"Oh, no," she cried hurriedly. "I am sure you would not. But I have known his family all my life."

"The fact remains," he cried stubbornly, "James FitzCharles is a spy and a murderer!"

"What?" The word flashed out suddenly, and they turned. Rachel stood at the door, her eyes wide, her cheeks as white as the lace at her throat.

Seven

Christian fell back upon his pillow, shuddering. Lucy cried, "Oh, you have frightened him into a faint. Where are the smelling salts? How white he is. . . ."

Rachel moved quietly across the room. She bent over Christian with the smelling salts. He coughed and turned his head away, his eyes beginning to water.

"There," Rachel said. "You are quite recovered." She drew a stool near to the bed and sat down, folding her hands in her lap. "Now, what is all this about James FitzCharles?"

Christian glanced at Lucy. "You may tell her," he shrugged in resignation.

Lucy poured the story out. Rachel listened with a sombre face, looking at Christian now and then, receiving a nod of silent confirmation at the more unbelievable points.

"It is incredible," she said at last.

"Just what I said," Lucy nodded. "Of course, he has a wild reputation. . . ."

"Not for treachery of this sort," Rachel said, her lips twisting curiously.

Christian lay back, shutting his eyes. Rachel looked at him closely. "He has talked far too much. I am come to relieve you. You have been sitting with him too long—go for a walk. You will have the headache if you do not take the air today."

Lucy hesitated. "You will not leave him alone?"

"Do not be such a goose," her aunt advised gently.

Lucy laughed. "Well, but if he was stabbed by someone at the Park it might be dangerous for him to be alone in case the murderer tries again."

"Very true," Rachel agreed. "So watch your tongue and do not mention a word of this to anyone."

Lucy sighed but obeyed. Tying her bonnet tightly, she set off down the lane at a brisk pace, meaning to walk as far as the Vicarage to hear the latest gossip in the village.

A great bay stallion suddenly leapt a hedge, some hundred yards away from her, and turned in her direction. With a sinking heart she recognized it as Hercules, a favorite mount of Mr. FitzCharles when he was at the Park.

He sat elegantly in the saddle, clothed in dove gray this afternoon, his boots polished so highly that they shone like mirrors. He saw her and drew rein, touching his hat.

"Good afternoon. It is Miss Lucy! How do you fare after your nocturnal excursion? What it is to be young and able to jaunt away the hours without ill effects."

The mocking drawl brought color flooding her cheeks. She gave him an angry glare, and tossed her head without deigning to reply.

After a pause, he added, "But for your own safety it would be wiser not to venture into the Park at such an hour again. . . ."

"Or you will murder me?" she flashed involuntarily, then bit her tongue in helpless dismay.

He stared. "What?" His face darkened. The thin

brows jerked together. "What do you mean by that?"

"It was a joke," she said hurriedly, falling over her words in her haste to propitiate him. "I am so sorry. Pray forgive me. . . ."

He swung down from the saddle, and took her by the elbow, staring into her white face.

"An odd sort of joke!"

"Let me go!" She cried out in terror.

"Good God, girl, I am not an ogre," he said, half amused, half angry. "What do you think I could do to you out here in daylight?"

She was half fainting, her face white. "Let me go!" She wrenched herself from his grasp and ran away. He followed more slowly, leading his horse, and tied it to the fence post.

His dark face was glowing with passionate anger. Her inexplicable behavior made him suppose that her aunt had fed her with high-flown tales of his libertine propensities, and despite his promise to his mother, his temper now had the upper hand.

Lucy tripped as she fled up the path, and by the time she had recovered herself and reached the door, he was on her heels. She thundered upon the door knocker, panting and sobbing. The door flew open, and she fell into Rachel's arms.

"I am sorry, I am sorry. I lost my head, and now he knows everything. . . ."

Rachel looked over her head. "What are you babbling about, you foolish child? We will begin to think you quite unhinged if you continue this way." She gave Mr. FitzCharles a cool smile. "I am sorry! She has read too many Gothic novels. You must pay her no heed."

He had himself more under control. "There is

something I must ask you," he murmured as coolly in reply, and advanced with the obvious intention of entering the house.

Short of struggling with him on her doorstep she was forced to step back. Lucy gave a wail of horror and fled away up the stairs out of sight.

Rachel followed him into the little front parlor where she found him standing beside the mantel shelf examining a small porcelain figure of a shepherdess, rather prettily painted in pastel colors. "Charming," he murmured. "We have a similar piece at the Park."

"I know," she said shortly. "That one was given to me by your Papa when he acquired his piece."

"He was very attached to you," he murmured.

She did not answer. After a moment, she asked, "You wished to ask me something?"

"I bear a message from my Mama," he agreed. "She wishes you and your nieces to visit us one evening for dinner. We would be very grateful. It is so long since you honored us."

"I am deeply honored, but I fear it will be impossible. . . ."

"Why?" he asked directly.

She sought desperately for an excuse. "I am afraid we have no suitable dress. We are so out of the world here, you know."

He turned then, his face bright with mocking amusement. "Oh, Rachel, you can do better than that!"

Her eyes sparkled angrily. "You force me to be frank, then. I could not consider dining at the Park."

"My Mama most earnestly wishes to see you there," he said.

"I am sorry." She held up her head, her chin defiant.

Like fencers circling each other, looking for an opening, they stared at each other.

He eventually reverted to the earlier topic. "You seem to have given your niece an odd idea of me. I did not suspect you saw me as Bluebeard."

Her brow wrinkled slightly. Her glance probed his face, and he stared back. As their eyes met his face seemed to glow with suppressed passion. Her heart quickened and she had to look away.

Suddenly there was a stumbling of feet in the passage, a cry from a girl's voice, and the door was flung open. Christian swayed in the doorway, hastily dressed in shirt and breeches, a pistol in his hand, leveled at Mr. FitzCharles.

Mr. FitzCharles looked astonished. Christian stared at him. The anger and hatred left his white face, and pure, blank astonishment filled his eyes. Rachel, watching them both with anxious intensity, could not be certain what she was watching.

"Mais, ce n'est pas lui," Christian stammered.

"What?" Lucy cried. "What did you say?"

"It is not him," Christian repeated. "It is certainly not Mr. FitzCharles." With a sigh of utter weariness he let the pistol fall from his limp fingers.

"You foolish, foolish boy," Rachel said. "Lucy, how could you let him do it? He is not up to such a venture."

As she spoke Christian slid down the doorpost to the floor. Mr. FitzCharles moved rapidly and caught him before he could hurt himself.

He lifted him as if he were a baby and glanced at Rachel. "Will you direct me to his room? I fancy he would do better in his bed."

"Yes," Rachel stammered. "Of course. This way." She led him up the stairs, Lucy following anxiously behind, observing with alarm the pallor of Christian's face, and the limp way in which he lay against Mr. FitzCharles.

Amelia's startled features appeared at the foot of the stairs, and Lucy heard her moan to Becky that she had known how it would be. They would all be ruined.

"Becky, bring up some camomile tea," Rachel commanded calmly. She watched Mr. FitzCharles lower the boy on to the bed and gently tuck the bedclothes over him.

Becky hurried into the bedroom with a mug of something pungent. Rachel lifted it to Christian's lips. He spluttered as the smell reached him, but she insisted that he drink some.

"Nom d'un nom," he spluttered. "What is it?"

"An herbal remedy," she smiled. "Will you take some more?"

"It is a poison of the rankest odor," he informed her. "What does she put into it? Bad eggs?"

"Herbs," Rachel assured him.

He grimaced. His eye fell upon Mr. FitzCharles, leaning at the foot of the bed with an urbane expression of cool curiosity. "Who is he?"

"It is Mr. FitzCharles," Lucy cried. "Oh, Rachel, is Christian out of his mind?"

Affronted, Christian drew himself up against the pillows. "I am perfectly sane, thank you! I never saw this man before in my life, though."

"But is he Mr. FitzCharles," Lucy urged anxiously.

Christian looked at Rachel. "It is so?"

She nodded.

Christian shrugged. "Then who was the other one? They must be brothers, I suppose." He yawned. "My faith, but my head aches. I cannot think. I am glad Lucy's fears were unfounded. . . ." He closed his eyes wearily, relaxing.

"We will leave you to sleep. Becky, stay with him. Lucy, go to your room and rest." Rachel looked at Mr. FitzCharles. "Will you come with me, sir?"

He followed her into the parlor again. She poured him a glass of elderflower wine. "I hope you will not dislike it too much," she apologized. "It is all I can offer you."

He looked warily at the glass of golden liquid. "Thank you," he murmured dubiously.

She laughed. "You need not look so. I promise not to poison you. Oh, are you remembering the remedy Becky gave poor Christian? Our wines are rather more palatable than that."

"I trust they are," he murmured.

"Craven!" Her eyes mocked him. "Will you not risk it?"

He raised the glass and sipped. An expression of surprise entered his face. "It is rather pleasant," he said.

She went to the kitchen to fetch some macaroons, and when she returned found him examining some books which lay on the table. He looked round, smiling. "I hope you will forgive my curiosity, but I am never able to see a book without examining it. It is an ill-bred habit."

"Indeed, it is not," she said. "I have it myself."

"I do not wish to cast aspersions upon your sex, Ma'am," he said gravely. "But it is unusual to find a female who enjoys reading Edward Gibbon."

"I find his rolling periods have a soothing effect," she replied.

"I am surprised that one of your parentage should entertain the idea of reading him, though."

"Oh, because he is against the clergy? Why, I discard a great deal of his private opinions. One can skim such a book with advantage."

He was watching her with an expression which made her flush. "You are unexpected, Rachel," he murmured. "First you harbor an escaped French prisoner. Now I discover you read Gibbon. I had not suspected you to be capable of either pursuit."

"I wondered if you would guess who he was," she said.

"I should be stupid if I had not," he retorted. "What is he doing in this house?"

"Lucy and Amelia found him in the Park last night."

"I should have guessed! What an abominable girl she is! But why did you give him shelter here?"

"He was so ill," she said. "I could not send word at such an hour, nor this morning could I allow him to be taken away in his present condition."

"How does he come to be wounded?"

She looked at him coolly. "He told us he was stabbed. By you."

"By me?" His brows rose steeply. "So that is the heart of the mystery! That is what Lucy meant?"

She sighed. "I must tell you the whole story."

"It would be as well," he agreed sardonically.

He listened as she explained, his face growing dark, and when she came to an end he rose and walked about with an angry step. At last he whirled to face her. "And you believed me to be a spy and a murderer?"

"Of course not," she said. "I did not know what to believe."

"But you had good reason for believing me capable of anything," he shot out. "Oh, my reputation! I knew you believe me a rake and a libertine, but this! It is intolerable!"

"I am sorry," she said unhappily.

His eyes flashed bitterly. "Sorry!" For a moment he looked more than capable of murder, then he drew a deep breath. "It is somewhat disconcerting to find oneself suspected of such deeds. I have spent much time and energy in building up my career." He smiled at her wryly. "Oh, I know you imagine I do nothing but pursue my pleasures, but I do take my career seriously, and this tale could ruin me."

"What will you do?"

"I have friends who will advise me," he said. "In the meantime we must really try to find this man who has been using my name as a cloak for his activities."

She looked at him uncertainly. "You have no idea who it could be?"

"None," he said in surprise, then shot her a sharp look. "Have you?"

"You are not the only one to bear the name Fitz-Charles," she said reluctantly.

He stared, then laughed loudly. "What, Freddy? Good God, no! Put the idea out of your head. It is impossible."

"It is something one should consider," she said gently.

"Not at all," he said. "I would as soon suspect my mother."

She laughed at that, and his eyes opened wide, as

though the sound delighted him. She sobered, looking shyly away. "What about Christian?"

"Can you keep him here for a while?" he asked. "I have an idea. It is obvious that the imposter is at the Park, but the accusation of a French prisoner of war will not carry much weight, without quite irrefutable proof of his story."

"No," she said. "I imagine not."

"We must identify the spy, but we must also make sure he gives himself away."

"How?"

"We will need a tethered goat," he said. "Live bait. Once our spy realizes that Christian is alive he will have to dispose of him before he can tell his story."

She shivered. "Oh, no!"

"I am afraid it is the only way," he said.

"I cannot allow you to use my house as a trap, and poor Christian as bait. He might kill the boy before we could stop him."

"I shall guard against such an eventuality," he said calmly.

"How would you do that?"

"My groom can stay in the house all night. He is a sensible fellow who knows how to hold his tongue. He can be trusted in any delicate situation."

"I am sure he can," she said sharply.

His eyes hardened. "Yes," he flung angrily. "He is normally called upon in more romantic situations, but you may depend upon him for your life. He can even cook and sew!"

"A paragon," she said dryly.

"What a shrew you are," he said in half mockery, half regret. "Milton will come down every evening and stay in the kitchen all night. Our spy will not make any attempt in daylight for fear of being seen."

"Oh, what a melodrama this sounds," she said in disbelief.

"You must take it seriously," he said. "You face real danger, I fear. I wish I could extricate you now, but I will see that you are well protected."

"I am not worried about myself," she said.

He spoke abruptly. "I am!"

She flushed, looked away, then walked towards the window. He watched her. After a moment he crossed to her side and stood gazing out upon the garden unseeingly.

"You must know how I hate to have you exposed to such danger," he said in a tightly controlled voice.

She did not answer. His nearness unsettled and disturbed her so that she had to close her eyes and avert her head. She had been fighting a losing battle against him for years. The last thing in this world I want, she thought, is for him to suspect how I feel. Her fiercely resisted weakness for him seemed to be increasing with each day.

While he was away she had half-forgotten him. Since his return she had had him continually on her mind, an irritant she could not soothe.

Wearily, seeing her so guarded, he said, "I will not trouble you by protestations, Rachel, but I beg you to reconsider the invitation to dinner. It would be the perfect opportunity for us to lure our traitor to your house without exposing either yourself or your nieces to danger."

"Yes, I can see that," she said carefully. "When do you suggest we come to you?"

"Tomorrow night? I will send my carriage, of

course, and make certain Milton is at your house before you leave it."

Her eyes suddenly lifted to his face. "I suppose it could not be Milton who . . ."

He laughed, looking less taut. "No, it could not! He is even less likely than my mother, if that is possible. If I had any suspicions of him at all do you think I would put your lives into his hands? I have had him with me all my life. He hates the French worse than poison."

She accompanied him to the door. In the porch hc paused, looking at her with that strangely weary expression, and her heart moved painfully in her breast. She held out her hand with a grave, reassuring smile. He took it in both his, looking into her eyes, and suddeny bent his head with a gesture of urgency and need, pressing his lips against her open palm. She trembled, her fingers jerking involuntarily. He immediately let her hand fall, bowed abruptly and walked away.

The early morning sunshine filtered down through the elms which fringed the lawn, piercing the shadowy recesses of the library, gilding the lettering on the spines of books, sliding over highly polished furniture and dusty shelves and pricking out with cruel clarity the lines of weariness on Mr. FitzCharles's handsome face.

His secretary, glancing up from his own work, was struck by the haggard appearance of his employer and asked, with some hesitation, if he had the headache.

"Headache?" Mr. FitzCharles looked up. "A slight one. I have not slept well these last few nights."

"Indeed, sir? I hope nothing is wrong?" The secretary said in his flat voice.

"Why should there be?" Mr. FitzCharles asked.

The secretary looked at him in some confusion. "If you are losing sleep, sir. . . ."

"You listen to gossip, I fear, my dear fellow," returned his employer lightly. "You must not believe all you hear."

Brown looked stolidly at him. "Sir?"

Mr. FitzCharles smiled sardonically. "I am not suffering from an excess of the tender passion, Brown."

"I did not imagine you were, sir," said the secretary tartly.

"No, it is not my style precisely," drawled Mr. FitzCharles.

"I was not intending to imply," began Brown.

"Excellent, Brown!" Mr. FitzCharles broke in, "Continue in this good intention. Have you ever considered how dangerous a good intention can be?"

Brown looked at him oddly. After a moment, he asked, "Shall we be returning to town when your guests leave, sir?"

The steady, cool gray eyes gazed at him. "I have no notion. Do you dislike the country, then?"

"The capital is more lively, sir."

"Ah, I suppose it is, though it has been lively enough here these past few days."

Brown loked blank. "Yes, sir?"

"That escaped prisoner, for instance," his employer said.

"The Frenchman, yes, that was out of the ordinary, I suppose," Brown said doubtfully.

"You are a master of the understatement,"

drawled Mr. FitzCharles. "Curious that he should have been wounded since he escaped."

"It is very strange, yes," Brown murmured.

"Perhaps he was caught in a man trap," Mr. FitzCharles said lightly.

Brown's eyes flashed open wide. "A man trap?" The words were jerked out of him in astonishment.

"The keepers set them for poachers, you know," replied his employer. "A cruel practice. I have forbidden it in the Park, but sometimes an old one is forgotten when it has been placed in some remote corner."

"No one has seen the Frenchman, though, sir," Brown reminded him.

Mr. FitzCharles nodded. "Odd, isn't it? Perhaps he died of his wound." He glanced at his secretary. The pale face was politely thoughtful as the other man looked back at him.

"Perhaps he did, sir," Brown agreed.

"Unless," Mr. FitzCharles continued softly, "unless this ridiculous rumor is true."

"Rumor about what, sir?"

"Oh, some foolish gossip Milton has brought back from the village ale house, but I cannot credit it. They believe that the prisoner is hidden in a house near here."

"Good heavens, sir!" Brown's eyes widened. "Who would hide a French prisoner of war? It cannot be so."

"Ah, that is the curious thing," said Mr. FitzCharles. "They would have us believe Miss Duncan has done so."

"Miss Duncan at the White House?" Brown looked at him sharply. "Indeed?"

Mr. FitzCharles rose with a yawn. "I am liverish

this morning. I'll take a stroll. What a remarkably efficient fellow you are, Brown. You have dealt with so much business this morning! You quite put me to shame."

"Thank you, sir."

"And I do not fancy your income would keep me in cravats," added Mr. FitzCharles wryly.

"I doubt it, sir," Brown agreed ironically.

"Quite so." The gray eyes smiled. "In which case it is doubly commendable in you to dress with such elegance. Your taste is excellent, but I hope all your worldly wealth is not upon your back, Brown."

The other man flushed.

"I do beg your pardon, my dear fellow. I approach the personal. In my clumsy way I am trying to introduce the subject of your salary. I think you merit a rise. Pray, see to it that I pay you another hundred pounds a year, Brown."

Brown looked both surprised and grateful, and stammered his thanks. Mr. FitzCharles waved them away.

"I am not being kind, Brown. I am facing facts. Let me recommend it as a pastime."

He had left the room before Brown could speak again. A few moments later the door opened. Looking up, the secretary saw Lady Danvers, her hair escaping from a primrose ribbon, her lips pouting. "Oh, it is only you, Brown! Where is your master?"

Brown grew even more pale than usual. "I am afraid he has this moment left the room, Lady Danvers."

"Do you know where he is gone?"

"He said he was going to walk in the park," he replied, his eyes sliding hungrily over her.

She saw the expression as they dwelt upon her

revealing neckline, and tossed her head indignantly. "Thank you," she said, in careful hauteur.

When she had gone Brown passed a hand over his pale face as if to expunge the shadow of some unwelcome emotion.

Mr. FitzCharles was joined in the park by his groom, Milton, who was a spare man with humorous eyes. "A quiet night, sir," he said softly. "I sat up into the small hours with the young gentleman. No visitors, though."

"You had better spend the day in bed. Give out that you've a bilious headache, and try to get some sleep."

"Thank you, sir."

"How is the Frenchman this morning?"

"Very sprightly," grimaced Milton. "Sitting up in bed singing French songs, sir."

"Reckless of him."

"So I told him, but he took not a scrap of notice until that Miss Lucy came screeching into the room. She stopped him."

"Ah," sighed Mr. FitzCharles. "The power of the female."

Milton winked. "Sweet on her, isn't he, sir? Come to that, she ain't backward in giving him a look or two." He stopped, looking over his master's shoulder, and his grin spread. "Lady Danvers coming over the lawn, sir," he said dryly.

Mr. FitzCharles gave him a repressive look. "Very well, Milton. That will do. Oh, and if you should get the chance, drop the word that you've heard gossip in the village about a Frenchman at the White House."

Milton's eyes rolled. "Oh ho! That's your game, is it?"

Isabella was a few feet away. Milton walked off as she cried, "James, why are you never where I want you? I have been searching for you, and that secretary of yours undresses me with his eyes as if I were the merest lightskirt. How I detest him!"

"Does he, indeed?" Mr. FitzCharles replied, lifting an eyebrow. "I had no idea his tastes ran in that direction."

"He makes my skin creep, I assure you. Such nasty little eyes, and so polite with it!"

"Is this why you have been searching for me?"

"No, how can you be so tiresome! It is Henry!" She sighed. "He is like a bear with a sore head this morning."

"I observed him in his cups last night," agreed Mr. FitzCharles. "It would follow. What has he been saying to you?"

"He is suspicious of you," she whispered, glancing over her shoulder with apprehension.

"He cannot hear us, my dear," he answered, with a gleam of amusement. "Now, do not be playacting."

"I am not! He hinted that he suspects us of . . . that we . . . I . . ."

"He suspects us of being lovers?" he supplied gravely.

"I wish you would not be so blunt," she said. "But, yes."

"I thought you were not anxious on his account," he teased.

She caught her lip between her teeth, looking very pretty and unhappy. "Well, I am," she cried defiantly. "My children mean a good deal to me, and I do not wish to lose Henry's respect!"

Gently, he said, "Then we must immediately allay his suspicions. Tell him you miss your children and wish to see them. He will understand that. Ask him when you are to go home, and show your eagerness to be with the children soon."

"Oh, if I were only home," she said miserably. "I wish I had never come here. Ever since that dreadful moment at the Temple I have been beside myself with anxiety."

"My fault entirely," he said soberly. "I take all blame."

"Well, I must say, I do wish you had not made such a dead set at me," she sighed. "It was such a temptation, you know. Henry is a good husband, but one could not call him exciting! London offered such pleasant diversions, but now I swear I am cured for all time of wishing to have what I never can again. From now on I will be a model wife!"

He laughed. "Do not be too reformed! You are too pretty!"

She automatically fluttered her lashes at him, then said, "James, you must try to desist from making me compliments. Is it any wonder I almost lost my heart to you?"

"You are right," he said. "I must guard my tongue. Tonight at dinner, by the way, we are expecting an addition to our party—two young ladies and their aunt."

"Of all things in the world I most abominate aunts," she said. "Sitting tatting in corners, gossiping."

"Not this aunt," he said, his eyes alight with something that was not just amusement.

She eyed him suspiciously. "Now what are you up to?"

"This aunt," he said, "Is an aunt I mean to marry—if I can!"

Eight

Putting Caesar on the leash, Mr. FitzCharles told him that he was expected to be on his very best behavior that day. "You are going to pay a courtesy call with me," he added gravely.

As they approached the White House he saw Lucy in the garden, her straw bonnet dangling by its wide ribbons. She smiled at him sunnily, clearly her fear of him evaporated once she knew he was not the villain who had attempted to kill Christian. Mr. FitzCharles grinned at her.

"How is our hero, today?"

"Much recovered," she said. "He has eaten some broth and is sitting up in bed."

"I have come to speak with your aunt," he said, turning towards the house.

"She is at the back of the house with Ralph," Lucy said, pointing to a horse cropping the grass nearby.

"Ralph Mellows?" inquired Mr. FitzCharles, preserving a polite expression by sheer effort of will. Rage had sprung up inside him like a forest fire, but he continued to smile. Even so Lucy shrank, puzzled, as she caught the odd glitter of the gray eyes.

"Yes," she stammered, wondering why he looked suddenly so odd. Then she recalled Ralph's strictures upon the FitzCharles family, and decided that Mr. FitzCharles must have been, at some time, in receipt of them.

Lucy had no fondness for Ralph Mellows. She smiled warmly at Mr. FitzCharles, admiring his wildly handsome good looks and elusive air of amusement, although the latter seemed oddly in abeyance at this moment.

"Shall we join them, then?" he asked tightly.

"Yes, let us do," Lucy nodded. "Ralph detests of all things to have us interrupt him when he is with Rachel."

"You do not like Mr. Mellows?" Mr. FitzCharles gave her a glance of surprised approval.

"I detest him," she announced frankly. "He is so patronizing. He treats me as though I were still in the nursery and he a graybeard."

"Your aunt, I gather, does not share your opinion of him?"

Lucy sighed. "No, and I can only suppose that at her age it is a comfort to have an admirer! I must be thankful she has not yet accepted him—to have him as one's uncle-in-law would be beyond everything!"

"He has offered for your aunt, then?" asked Mr. FitzCharles, only too well aware of the impropriety of discussing such a subject with a young female of Lucy's tender years, yet unable to resist discovering how much of a rival Ralph Mellows was likely to be.

"Oh, yes," Lucy groaned. "We live in daily fear she will accept!"

"I see," he said grimly.

She led him round the side of the house to where a rose-heavy trellis screened off the rest of the garden, which ran down to the Park, some two hundred yards away.

Suddenly he caught Rachel's soft voice. "So you have had Jeb Smith up before you again, Ralph."

"Yes, he was out again, bold as brass, with a bag of rabbits and my pheasants. He'll end up like his father, transported or hung! Why will they poach?"

"The children go hungry, Ralph, and a rabbit or two would not be missed, surely?"

Ralph was curt. "It is the principle of the thing!" Rachel moved, and Mr. FitzCharles saw the shimmer of her white gown through the sun-dazzling green leaves of the roses. They heard the click of scissors, and a rustle of skirts. Then Ralph spoke again, in an altered voice. "Rachel, what answer am I to have?"

She sighed. "Oh, Ralph, my dear friend. . . ."

Eagerly he moved nearer. "Tell me it is yes," he pleaded.

Lucy looked uneasily at Mr. FitzCharles, scenting some puzzling emotion in him as he listened. When she would have interrupted, he caught her wrist in a grip of iron, glaring at her to be still. She drew in her breath with pain, her long skirt blowing in the wind, and Rachel caught the sound.

"Who is there?" she cried. "Who is that?"

Mr. FitzCharles released Lucy and she rubbed her arm, giving him an indignant look as she walked into the garden.

He followed her, strolling under the rose-hung arch on to the narrow path. Rachel looked at him coolly, then at Lucy.

"Lucy, take Mr. FitzCharles's dog into the kitchen and give him a drink," she ordered.

Lucy reluctantly obeyed, leaving the two men facing each other in the sunlit garden. Ralph, upon close inspection, was remembered by Mr. FitzCharles to be a stunted youth, a mere five feet five inches high, sturdily but inelegantly built, with broad shoulders and heavy calves, wearing ill-fitting garments of tasteless hue. His short, curly hair had the appearance of having been cut by himself. His bright blue eyes blazed with all the challenge of youth, His worst fault, perhaps, was that he stood beside Rachel giving out an atmosphere of proprietary jealousy. Mr. FitzCharles did not take to him.

Rachel performed polite services, remembering them to each other, quite unnecessarily, since each knew perfectly well who the other was, and each wished the other a hundred miles away.

Ralph endeavored to give the impression that he was, in all but name, master of the house, and Mr. FitzCharles with arrogant courtesy gave him to understand that he was nothing but a country squire out of place in polite society.

Rachel gave them both a coolly reproving look, and intervened to separate them before they came to downright discourtesies. Lucy came out into the garden again in time to see Ralph being led away to find his horse, and she gave Mr. FitzCharles a grin.

"That was well done. You have driven him off! I hope he does not too soon return!"

"So do I," he returned bluntly, and they both laughed.

Rachel spoke in a voice like a whip. "Lucy! Go into the house, if you please, and see if Christian needs anything!"

Lucy jumped, going pink, and scurried into the house without a backward glance. Rachel stared at Mr. FitzCharles.

"You should not have teased Ralph in that fashion," she reproved quietly.

"Had the young puppy spoken to me so in any other company I should have had great pleasure in demanding satisfaction," he said harshly. "As it was, I swallowed the insult of his tone, and he walked away whole, for which he has you to thank."

"You mistake his character if you imagine he would be thankful to escape a duel. He is a great fire-eater. and would have been very happy to meet you."

"His manners are appalling," he said curtly.

"The Mellows estate was considerable once, you know, and Ralph feels cheated when he feels the difference in his social standing which the possession of all that land would have made."

"Then he should look for a rich wife," Mr. Fitz-Charles drawled.

Her color deepened. "You were listening!"

"I wished to hear your answer. What would it have been, Rachel? Do you mean to accept him?"

She was arranging roses in the basket, white ones, just opening from the bud, the center golden with pollen, the petals thick and waxen. Suddenly she cried out, putting her finger in her mouth.

"Have you pricked yourself?" He took her finger and looked at the small red mark.

"The thorn is still embedded. Stand still. I will extract it for you." he gently withdrew the thorn, and then with a gesture kissed her finger. "There! I have made it better!"

For a second they stared at each other. Her eyes were wide and dark with emotion. He moved involuntarily nearer, a hungry look in his eyes.

Trembling, she turned and began to pick roses, blindly, with shaking fingers. The roses were overpoweringly fragrant, the larkspur swayed in the wind, towered over by huge yellow sunflowers whose dark centers looked like black eyes watching them. Heat seemed to rise from the ground as the morning wore on to noon.

"Do you mean to accept Mellows?" he asked her again, watching her.

"Ralph is the only other being in the world who has a right to an answer to that question," she said calmly, having recovered her self control. "Do not ask me."

"I think I would kill him if you did," he said without emphasis.

For a moment she thought she had misheard him, then she turned and looked at him in grave disapproval which masked the first, involuntary leap of passionate response her heart had given. "You must not say such things."

He looked haggard, his gray eyes blazing at her. "Do not be prim with me, Rachel. For you to marry that bumpkin would be a sin against your heart."

The window above them opened and Christian leaned out, smiling. "Good morning!"

Mr. FitzCharles gave a ragged sigh of irritation, but looked up to reply politely, "You look much recovered today, my dear Touslain."

"You see me growing very bored with these four walls," Christian nodded. "My pretty jailer will not allow me to set foot on the stairs, but I feel very fit."

"She is wise," Mr. FitzCharles said. "Any chance caller might catch you."

Christian leaned down to reply, but the glass of the open window shattered with a loud crack, and he jumped back out of sight with an involuntary movement.

"Oh, good God!" cried Rachel. "What has happened?"

Mr. FitzCharles ran through the garden, towards the park palings which marked the division of the land, and climbed over into a plantation of young saplings. He saw no one, and heard nothing. Then he suddenly caught the sound of twigs cracking from the left, and followed, weaving between the slender young trees. In a while he found himself coming out into the open spaces of the park. He halted, staring.

Far ahead of him, strolling along with a gun over his arm, was his brother Freddy, a gun dog at his heels and his head thrown back in cheerful contemplation of the morning.

Mr. FitzCharles stared after him for a moment or two, then glanced across at the Temple, having caught a sudden impression of a furtive movement in the shadowy recesses of the building.

When he quietly approached it he found his cousin George standing on the stone mosaic floor, staring with amused interest at the naked marble bodies which lined the walls.

"Hello, George. What are you doing? Worshipping Diana?"

George glared at him. "I'm attempting to conceal myself from your Mama. She will persecute me."

Mr. FitzCharles laughed. "Will she, indeed?"

George looked sulky. "She has some wild notion that Elizabeth is in love with some other fellow and wants me to give her up. I don't see why I should. She accepted me, didn't she?"

What has Mama been up to now, thought Mr.

FitzCharles. Aloud, he said, "Have you spoken to Elizabeth about this?"

George went a dark red. "No, and I shall not! If I bring it up, damn it, I shall have to give her the chance to break the engagement, and why should I be jilted? It would be cursed embarrassing."

"But, surely, George, if she is attached to someone else?"

"It is probably someone quite ineligible," George said sullenly. "Why else should she accept me otherwise?"

"Do you think it kind to marry her without first discovering the state of her emotions?" Mr. FitzCharles suggested gently.

George's brow darkened. "Do you really think I should speak to her?"

With some curiosity, his cousin asked, "Can it be that you are sincerely attached to Elizabeth, George?"

George kicked at the floor childishly. "She's a very soothing sort of girl. At first I did not wish to marry anyone, but one gets accustomed to ideas, you know, James, and if one must marry it is no bad thing to marry a girl who does not always nag at one to do things for her."

Hard put to it not to laugh, Mr. FitzCharles said, "She is a very charming girl, I quite agree, and if I were you I should make a push to secure my interest with her. You do not pay her enough attention, you know. It would not be surprising if she looked elsewhere for the little kindnesses females seem to need."

George thought slowly about this. "Well," he said at last, with a different stare, "Well, I will not ask her outright if she has a preference for someone else. I will just bring up the subject tactfully. After all, James, she might think I was trying to jilt her if I went at it like a bull at a gate."

"Very true," Mr. FitzCharles agreed soberly. "By the way, my dear fellow, have you seen anyone come out of the plantation while you have been here?"

"That cursed Freddy," George said crossly. "He waved to me, damn him! I only hope he does not inform your Mama that I am here."

Mr. FizCharles laughed and left him. When he returned to the White House he found the whole household in Christian's room. The young Frenchman was propped up in bed with a pile of pillows. The assembled company turned to greet Mr. FitzCharles with eager cries of curiosity.

"Did you see who it was?"

He shook his head. "I followed him back to the Park, but he managed to escape." Crossing to the window he examined the glass. "You had a fortunate escape," he told Christian. "I had not expected him to be so bold during the day. It would be as well for you to remain out of sight. No more leaning out of windows."

Christian looked smug. "I saw the flash of the powder before it actually hit the window. It is fortunate my nerves are so good."

"Oh, that wicked, wicked man," burst out Lucy, her eyes bright with rage.

"It is a pity that he saw me here," Mr. FitzCharles murmured thoughtfully. "Now he knows that I have spoken to you. He will be doubly on his guard. The question is—will he risk all by another attempt? Or try to escape at once? Or, if he is really intelligent, lie low and do nothing, realizing that no court would convict an Englishman on the evidence of a French prisoner of war?"

"Face it out?" Rachel sighed. "That would be very hard, surely, unless he has nerves of steel."

"He will have much to contend with," Mr. Fitz-Charles agreed. "There will be scandal. People may well thing that there is no smoke without fire. Even if he is not brought to court, there may be social consequences for him to face."

Rachel watched him. "You do know who it is, do you not?"

He looked at her somberly, shrugging. Lucy gave an excited cry of curiosity. "Who? Who?"

Teasingly, Mr. FitzCharles pinched her chin. "You sound like an owl!"

He walked towards the door. "I must get back before I am missed. My guests already complain that I neglect them."

Lucy giggled, and Rachel looked crossly at her. Mr. FitzCharles inwardly cursed himself for having mentioned the subjct which must recall to Rachel's mind the incident her nieces had witnessed in the moonlight two nights since.

When he had gone, Lucy burst out, "I do not wish to dine at the Park tonight! I will not leave poor Christian to be murdered in his bed! I could not eat a morsel for thinking about it! As to laughing and talking with a set of fellows, anyone of whom may be the man who has twice tried to kill Christian, well, all I can say is—it is beyond the bounds of decency!"

"Moderate your tone, Lucy," Rachel chided gently. "You must not speak so wildly."

"Oh, Rachel, indeed I could not pretend! I should betray all in a moment."

"She would, too," Becky grunted. "Never did have any self control!"

"Then it is high time she learnt some," Rachel said firmly. "I am shocked to hear you boast of giving way to your feelings, Lucy. It is pure selfishness. You have not considered that Amelia and I could not go out tonight knowing that we had left you behind in such danger! It is bad enough that we must leave Christian, but he is a man!"

Lucy was looking unhappily at her, her head hanging.

Rachel went on quietly. "Milton could not be expected to protect both of you, could he? You were brave enough to go adventuring in the Park at night. Surely you can command nerve enough to sit through one meal without indulging in melodramatics?"

"You do not understand," Lucy wailed.

"I understand only too well," Rachel informed her. "You must learn to control yourself, child. You know why we are going to the Park tonight. We wish to give Christian's enemy the impression that the house is empty so that he may make another attempt upon his life, and Milton may catch him in the act. We cannot permit you to spoil it all."

Lucy looked at Christian wildly. "Do you agree with her?"

Gently, he said, "I am afraid I do, Lucy. I can be brave for myself, but I could not be easy knowing you were in danger, too."

Lucy sighed. "Very well," she capitulated.

Nine

Rachel sat before her mirror, staring in dissatisfaction at the long, straight lines of her fashionable azure silk. She had bound her smooth hair with a matching fillet, but she could not help wishing most earnestly that she wore the Grecian curls which were currently all the rage.

"I am become a dowd!" she murmured to herself. "I must really make a stir to spend a few weeks in Bath in the autumn, for my own sake as much as for the sake of the girls. There is really no reason why I should not follow fashion, even if I do live out of the world here for most of the year."

Brought up in the quiet of a Christian household Rachel had been taught to measure the world by exacting standards. She firmly disapproved of the morality current in the upper classes. Mild flirtation between the eligible young was one thing. For it to continue after marriage was quite another.

From her corner of England she had observed the craze for excitement taken to shameful lengths. The war had intensified the wild balls, the gaming, the affairs conducted publicly and without shame. It was not the sort of life Rachel wished to lead. She could not help but be shocked.

At Temple Warren she had a place in the life of the village. She had duties to perform, a gentle routine to follow, and if life was sometimes a trifle dull, well, she had decided that it was better to be dull than to ruin one's life in the mad pursuit of pleasure.

When James FitzCharles inherited his father's estates Rachel met him again, after some years of absence, with a certain reserve. His father had been kind to her, she had heard him so many times deplore his elder son's way of life, and had inwardly agreed with him that it was a great pity James could not give up his desire for a public career in order to come home and tend his own estate.

"Absentee landlords are the devil," old Mr. Fitz-Charles had grunted. "The land decays under 'em. Stewards get ideas. The tenants grow surly and discontented. James should come home. Let Freddy take up a career if one of them is to do so—although I cannot imagine what he would do. Poor boy's a fool." He had scowled with disappointment at the leaping fire. "Damn James! He has his place here. Why can't he be content with it?"

The old man died, and James came home at last. But not, it soon appeared, to remain. Merely to tie up the loose ends of the estate, install a bailiff to manage the business, and cast a lordly but indifferent eye over all that now belonged to him.

Rachel, hearing Mr. Bailey, the bailiff, bewail his new master's dismaying lack of interest in his estate, had grown antagonistic to James before they ever met again.

His mother had brought him to the White House on a duty call. He had not seen Rachel for years. He had stalked in, dark and bored, his handsome face showing all his resentment of the fact that he was here at all, and then there had been a flash from the cold gray eyes, as if lightning had shot across the room, and his whole face altered. Rachel did not know that at that instant of meeting, James FitzCharles had fallen in love.

She was, however, surprised that he stayed as long as he did, and even more surprised when he returned with increasing frequency, showering her with invitations to visit his house.

His mother appeared as astonished as Rachel herself, but smiled upon this new development, having an old fondness for the girl which made it possible for her to overlook Rachel's lack of fortune.

Even Rachel's dislike for Mr. FitzCharles could not hide from her for long that he was making her the object of ardent and decided attentions. She supposed, with great anger and resentment, that he thought her so lacking in opportunities in the marital field that she would fall like a ripe plum into his hands. It did not so much as cross her mind in an idle moment that he might be seriously considering marriage. She imagined his intentions to be rather less than honorable.

She held him at arm's length, attempting by coldness and chilling courtesy to show him her reactions to his pursuit of her, and then he called one day, with a suppressed and passionate glow in his gray eyes, and after a few idle remarks about the weather, amazed and disconcerted her by plunging into a proposal of marriage.

Rachel had taken this to be the reaction of a vain and spoiled man, used to conquest, who finds himself unable to achieve his ends by any other means and is pushed, by a desire for his own way, to the ultimate attempt.

She had refused him, coolly, politely but without hesitation, and without any sign of softening.

His face had whitened, his gray eyes grown dark.

He had looked at her as if she had slapped his face, in disbelief. If anything could have hardened her attitude this incredulity at her refusal was it. He stammered a demand that she enlighten him as to her reasons for refusing him.

With a frosty look she told him, "When I marry it will not be a man like yourself—a gamester, a rake, a libertine. Such men should never marry and burden women with their presence. . . ."

His mouth had opened and shut for a moment. He thought, she saw, that his ears had deceived him. Then a slow rage dawned in his face. He glared at her, grasped her by the shoulders and kissed her ruthlessly and long. Rachel had never in her life been kissed in such a fashion. A few chaste salutes, stolen in secret at balls, had not prepared her for the revelation of so physical an emotion.

When he had done, he walked out of the room without another word, leaving her white-faced, a hand to her bruised mouth, facing a truth from which his kisses had wrenched the veils—her cool indifference to him had been assumed. Her real feelings were very different.

Time had helped her to resume those veils. She did not regret her decision. Even supposing his love to be genuine she was sure that it could not last. When he grew weary of domesticity he would return to his old pleasures, and she would be left to regret her mistake. Her pride would be wounded, her heart twisted at each new betrayal. She had seen too many fashionable marriages to wish to lead such a life.

She had closed the incident by putting him out of her mind and taking up the quiet threads of her life with renewed vigor. Her repsonsibilities had given her so much to do that she had not time to mourn a lost chance.

She sighed, gazing into the mirror.

His return had been inopportune. Ralph's proposal had been one she might possibly accept. Certainly with him she would never need to be anxious about his way of life. Ralph was eager to be moulded into a husband. Conventional, kindly, a little sulky at times, he would make a good partner for any woman prepared to carry more than her share of the relationship. Love did not only mean a violent emotion. Affection meant a great deal. She was fond of Ralph, enjoyed his company and knew that Mellows House was a pleasant, comfortable home. Women had married with far less reason.

She looked at herself again, sighing. Since James returned her mind had been confused, uncertain. She told herself that nothing was altered. That first night, at the Temple, the girls had seen him making love to some female. Yet he claimed to be in love with her! How could he bc?

Lucy burst in, gracefully coltish in her white muslin, her curls tied with a blue ribbon. "Oh, Rachel," she said, coming to a stop, staring at her aunt. "You look so elegant!"

"Thank you, Lucy," her aunt said, amused by the girl's utter astonishment.

"I have never seen you look so in countenance," Lucy added excitedly. "Oh, Milton is here and so is the carriage to take us to the Park."

Milton was toasting his boots at the fire in the kitchen, a jug of mulled ale swinging close to his elbow on a hot plate suspended above the flames.

He stood up when Rachel came into the room and wished her good evening, his eyes frankly admiring the picture she made in her blue dress. The color in her cheeks, and the brightness of her eyes, made her look a girl again.

Becky was ordered to lock herself in her room as soon as the carriage had left. "Pray, do as I bid you," Rachel insisted. "I cannot do without you, as you very well know."

Becky looked grimly flattered.

In the carriage Rachel was aware of a quivering excitement deep inside her. She had not been to a party for so long that she imagined herself to be beset by anticipatory pleasure.

They were welcomed to the house by the butler, who smiled upon Rachel with approval, having known her all her life, and murmured discreetly that, knowing she was to be present, the cook had included her favorite dish—a ham, baked in pastry, flavored with cinnamon and crumbled brown sugar, mustard and sliced apple.

"How delightful," Rachel said. "Pray, thank her for me. I shall look forward to tasting it." She laughed. "She knows I have never been able to make it half so good. My sauce is either too rich or too thick."

When she was announced, Mrs. FitzCharles came towards her with delight, kissing her upon both cheeks. "And Lucy and Amelia, too—this is a pleasure, my dears." In their pretty white muslins they made their demure curtsey, and were kissed, in their turn, then they were introduced to the other guests.

Rachel was puzzled by the wide eyes of her nieces as they were introduced to Lady Danvers, but supposed her beauty and elegance to have impressed them.

Mr. FitzCharles, leaning languidly back in a fragile gilt chair, watched Rachel's face intently as she was presented to Lady Danvers, but saw no betraying awareness.

The butler announced dinner. They all rose to go in, and as the party was formed into pairs, Lucy seized the opportunity to whisper to Rachel. "Lady Danvers is the female whom we saw with Mr. FitzCharles at the Temple! Imagine it! Is it not shocking, for she is a married woman!"

She was then claimed by Mr. Brown, the secretary, who was to take her in to dinner, and went off before she could see the effect this revelation had had upon her aunt.

Rachel was taken in upon Sir Henry's arm, behind his sister and Mr. FitzCharles, while Freddy brought up the rear with Amelia.

"Duncan," said Sir Henry in gruff but pleasant tones. "I believe I am familiar with the name. I was up at Oxford with a Duncan—a John Filden Duncan, took the cloth later, I recall."

"My father!" Rachel smiled at him. "He was vicar of this parish. He died a year ago."

"Very sorry to hear it," he replied sincerely. "I would have liked to meet him again."

She looked at him in pity. Poor man, he doubtless had no notion that his beautiful wife was unfaithful to him with his host. How could such a thing happen? Here they all sat, the host smiling, Lady Danvers looking as if she had nothing on her conscience, and Sir Henry eating his baked ham with the best appetite in the world: three corners of a deadly and treacherous triangle.

Rachel wanted no part of such a social life. It was like a glittering, sunlit pond; on the surface so beautiful, but underneath dwelt a thousand venomous insects, killing and being killed, living in mud and slime and feeding one upon the other.

Freddy and Amelia appeared to have struck up a curious friendship. Rachel could hear Amelia, lively with interest, laughing, and wondered what Freddy could be saying to her to make her so unusually vivacious. It was rare for Amelia to be so at ease in company. She was always so stiff and unhappy when she felt herself among strangers.

Catching her eye, Freddy turned to smile at her, leaning forward to say confidentially, "Charming girl, your niece. So easy to talk to. Not many girls make it so easy for one, you know."

"What have you been discussing so ardently?" she asked, smiling at him.

"I have been telling her about an amazing dwarf I saw in town," he confided. "No higher than a five-year-old child, but talked amazingly. Not language fit for a lady, though," he added thoughtfully. "It was the most wonderful thing, I can tell you, to see him take off a bottle of port as if it were milk."

"So I should imagine," Rachel murmured, catching Mr. FitzCharles's eye at that moment, and involuntarily responding to the silent amusement of his gray eyes.

"I wish I could escort your niece to see it," Freddy mourned. "She'd find it highly interesting. Should you like to see it?"

Rachel politely expressed a desire never to see it, adding that personally she did not really much care for such sideshows as dwarfs, giants or india rubber men.

Freddy conferred upon her a pitying look, and resumed his conversation with Amelia.

"How could you pass up such an opportunity?" drawled James FitzCharles. Rachel gave him a cool look, turned her shoulder delicately and began a long conversation with Sir Henry upon the latest theory of the rotation of crops, a topic much discussed in the farming circles of the neighborhood.

When the ladies withdrew Rachel found herself seated beside Lady Danvers, who was clearly curious about her. Rachel found it extremely embarrassing, seeing her companion knew something of her relationship with Mr. FitzCharles, and knowing what she did of his very different relations with Lady Danvers.

The gentlemen did not long withold their company, but it seemed to Rachel a dragging time, for she had to make polite small talk under intolerable conditions.

The night was very warm. Hardly a breath stirred the heavy brocade curtains hanging at the long windows, standing wide open to catch the faintest breeze. The ladies fanned themselves and sighed. It was not long before Lucy, daringly, suggested that they take a walk in the garden by moonlight, an idea which made Mrs. FitzCharles look quite shocked, but which Freddy leapt at with delight.

"May we, Rachel?" Amelia pleaded. "I am stifling hot, and it would be so delightful. . . ."

Mr. FritzCharles spoke enthusiastically. "I think it a prime idea! We might one evening have a moonlight picnic! After all, Mama, there is no need to look so horrified! How many times have we been to Vauxhall by moonlight, and danced and supped al fresco with the city gentry? What is so different about a stroll in our own garden?"

Freddy took Amelia and Lucy upon his arm and, laughing gaily, the three of them vanished into the shadowy garden. Lady Danvers caught Mr. FitzCharles's eye and said, a little regretfully, "I do not think I have the energy for strolling. Henry, shall we sit down at the card table with Mrs. FitzCharles and Mr. Brown?"

Sir Henry looked gratified. Mr. Brown was obsequiously polite, leaping at once to open the card box for them and arrange the chairs.

James FitzCharles looked at Rachel.

"Will you allow me to show you the Temple?"

She was astounded by his audacity. "I shall not walk in the garden, thank you," she said coldly.

"I wish to speak to you more privately than our present company would permit," he murmured for her own ears, alone. "There can be no question of your being compromised, you know," he added wickedly, with a teasing look. "Your nieces are out there with my brother, after all."

She flushed, but assented, and allowed him to place her hand upon his arm.

The moon shone unclouded tonight above the scented rows of flower beds, dancing whitely over the waters of the lake and turning to silver everything that moved, trees, flowers, the windvane on top of the old stable.

"It does not appear that our friend the spy will make an attempt tonight," he murmured at her elbow "No doubt he smells the trap. The fox has an uncanny nose for the stopped up earth."

She looked up at him searchingly. "You will not tell me whom you suspect?"

"You are amazingly discreet, for a female," he said, "But your glance might betray you. Could you pretend ignorance when you once knew who it was?"

She laughed bitterly. "I think I have been discreet tonight," she said.

A little silence. He drew in a sharp breath. "Ah! Your nieces reconized my companion at the temple?"

"Did you expect they would not?"

"I hope they will be discreet," he said.

"A pity you were not," she snapped.

"Rachel, it was not what you imagine! A little light flirtation, nothing more! Is one kiss to be labeled an act of infidelity?"

"Has Sir Henry Danvers no right to expect that his wife will keep her kisses for him only? How would you view such behavior in your wife? If she were caught in another man's arms at night?"

"I would be tempted to kill them both," he admitted in a low tone.

"Let us hope Sir Henry is less savage," she said coolly. "He is a good man. I am sorry for him."

"Rachel," he appealed, "Consider! Isabella is your own age. She was only just out when she married Sir Henry, a mere girl—and he was almost twice her age. It was no love match, on either side. Her family arranged it. Sir Henry wanted her because she was the most beautiful girl of the season. She obeyed because she had no choice."

"That does not excuse her weakness," she said briefly.

"You should not judge everyone by your own standards," he said in bitter tones. "Most of us are more fallible."

She felt the chill of virtue upon her skin, and shivered. She had no wish to sit in judgment on others. She had spoken out of her own hurt.

After a moment, she said, "Do not be anxious. I will do what I can to shield Lady Danvers from discovery, and I will see that my nieces do the same."

"Thank you," he said, watching her face with darkened eyes.

She bent over a rose bush, touching the white flowers with fingers that trembled slightly. "Your staff keep the gardens in great beauty. It is a shame that there is rarely anyone to see the effects of their work."

"You come in from time to time, I gather," he said. "If the roses bloom only for your eyes they justify all the work spent on them."

She flushed and turned away. He was too persuasive, altogether, with that cool, strong voice which gave no hint of the disgraceful pleasure he loved to pursue. She was determined to be unyielding.

"Keep your pretty speeches for Lady Danvers," she said in icy tones.

"My dear girl," he drawled. "If I did not know you so well I would put that remark down to pure jealousy!"

She was instantly enraged. "How dare you! I! Jealous of you! You flatter yourself."

She was shamefully aware of disappointment. The effect of the moonlight, and their romantic surroundings, combined with the heady wine she had taken at dinner, had made her pulses race while he was so close to her. She would have rejected one of his attempts to win her over, but she felt illogically stung because he had not made one.

Of course, she thought, his pursuit of her was a mere whim! She could not expect anything more—but it was not flattering that, having been alone with her for so long in such a setting, he had ignored his opportunity.

"Shall we go back?" she asked.

"I have not told you my news," he said quickly. "I have written to London, to a friend of mine who deals in these matters, and he is coming down here, I hope, to investigate this business. It is no good leaving these things to local magistrates. They have no useful experience of anything more interesting than poaching."

"Then I hope your spy does not stir out of his hole until your friend arrives," she said tightly.

"I hope he does," he said. "Unless we have such proof I am going to have a hard time convincing everyone of my innocence."

George, meanwhile, led Elizabeth around the rim of the lake, pointing out smugly that the moon shed a brilliant light over the Temple. "The Temple affords a romantic prospect by moonlight," he said, quoting from a local guidebook he had read up that very afternoon for the purpose.

Elizabeth smiled. She recognized this as a quotation, and was touched that he should have bothered to learn it on her behalf.

George looked at her, and stammered, "I say, Elizabeth . . . you . . . you don't object to marrying me, do you? I mean to say, there is nobody else, is there?"

She gave him a shimmering, radiant smile. "No one else, George," she admitted shyly.

He breathed relief. "And you don't mind marrying me?"

"No," she said softly, lowering her eyes.

George, inspired for the first and only time in his life to a romantic gesture, put his hand to the curve of her cheek. "You know what, you have very pretty eyes," he said clumsily.

She lifted them, her lips parted on a sigh of sheer happiness. George, having exhausted his fount of compliments, bent forward and kissed her. At once her arms came up round his neck, and she kissed him back so enthusiastically as to astonish him. Filled with confidence George clapsed her closer, and thought to himself that, for once, his aunt Fitz-Charles had been in the wrong of it. He did not know how she came to be so foolish, but he mentally composed a stinging rebuke which when next they met would prove to her how little she understood young females. Then, finding Elizabeth's lips warm and deliciously yielding, he forgot his aunt and her strange belief that Elizabeth was unhappy, and concentrated on enjoying the fleeting moment.

When they were in the carriage on their way home Rachel was suddenly overcome with a conviction that they would find Milton lying in a pool of blood in the kitchen, and Christian and Becky shot dead in their beds.

The consequent relief, when Milton opened the door to them all, was considerable.

Lucy clamored for news of Christian, and Rachel bade her be quiet and go to bed. Milton grinned at them. "Not a mouse stirred," he assured them. "Our piece of cheese had its supper, played cards with me for an hour or two, then went off to sleep as natural as a baby."

"I will just look in upon him to make certain," Lucy said, creeping off.

"You will do nothing of the kind," Rachel said sharply. "Go straight to your own bed, Miss!"

Milton looked at her furtively, reading his own story into the weariness and irritation in her eyes. She had probably quarreled with the master again, he thought. What a pair! They were old enough to know better. This Tweedle-dum and Tweedle-dee stuff was for children, not a man and woman in the prime of life.

Ten

There was a light mist masking the downs next morning, and throughout the day a thin drizzle fell at intervals, confining Rachel and her nieces to the house, and lending a gray light to the whole landscape.

Rachel was unaccountably irritable from her first waking thought, which happened to be of a certain expression seen fleetingly in Mr. FitzCharles's eyes as he put her into the carriage, which image she sought to banish by energetic pursuit of household tasks.

Becky, chivied through a totally unnecessary program of domestic rearrangement, grumbled to herself softly as she went about the house, venting her own irritation in words.

When the house was straight again, Rachel announced firmly, "It is time to make the green tomato chutney. We must begin before the tomatoes spoil."

The kitchen was soon full of the rich odors of onion, tomato and herbs, the smell even penetrating to the parlor, where Amelia sat over a tapestry she had been making for two years, but which had never progressed beyond the central figure of Britannia uneasily wielding what looked more like a pitchfork than a trident. This vast concept, involving a ship of the line in full sail, a portrait of George III in profile which made him look like a florid turnip, and a great many wavy blue lines intended to indicate the sea, had been occupying Amelia for most of her spare time.

She and Lucy had begun tapestries together, but Lucy had long ago unpicked what she had done and used the silks to make a formal garden of pansies and roses with which to ornament the chair seats in the parlor.

Lucy had spent most of the day with Christian, ready aloud to him from a slim volume of poems. He listened, his dark eyes riveted upon her face.

Rachel was uneasily aware that it was not wise for the girl to spend so much time alone with the romantic young Frenchman, but she did not like to put too much emphasis upon the delicacy of the situation, for fear of putting into Lucy's head ideas not already there.

Her romantic and vigorous nature would always, Rachel knew, expose her to more temptation than would ever be the case with her sister, and, although Rachel had come to like and trust Christian, she knew how impossible must be any possibility of a marriage between them.

As the day wore on, Rachel was increasingly inclined to snap. She had half-expected either a visit or a message from the Park, and when none was forthcoming felt a curious urge to burst into tears. She went into her own chamber and stared at herself critically in the glass. The fresh bloom of the previous evening had gone. The brightness had deserted her eyes, the mist had taken the gloss from her hair and discontent had given a droop to her mouth.

When Milton arrived that evening she went into the kitchen to speak to him, ostensibly to ask if there had been any developments at the Park.

Milton, observing her shrewdly, saw that the

same expression of tense anticipation filled her eyes as he had seen in his master's that morning.

She asked him if Mr. FitzCharles expected the traitor to try again to kill Christian.

"Well, you see how it is, Ma'am," Milton said. "Once the young gentleman is up and able to walk, he can come to the Park and pick the spy out. Although that ain't proof what would convince an English jury, you may be certain mud would stick, and this fine gentleman wouldn't want mud on his coat."

Rachel sighed. "But to kill! It is shocking."

"He has tried twice to kill him, Ma'am," Milton reminded her. "He may think third time lucky!"

She shivered. "Well, we must hope that this whole business is soon safely over." She hesitated. "I suppose this weather has confined the house party indoors, Milton?"

"It has, Miss Rachel. They have been playing cards and squabbling like children. My master attended to business most of the day." He shot her a shrewd glance. "He sent his especial regards, Miss," he added confidentially.

She flushed, gave him a cold glance and withdrew with great dignity.

Milton winked at Becky. "Fair mad about your young lady, he is, you know."

"If you want a tankard of ale," Becky said tartly, "get it yourself." She went on rubbing spoons vigorously with a piece of soft kid.

"I won't say no, thank you kindly," Milton said, unabashed by her brisk tone. "Sir Henry is wanting to visit the earthworks at Dover Castle but Mr. James doubts as how they'll get permission. That's military property, he says, and 'ighly confidential."

"Earthworks!" Becky sniffed, breathing on a spoon. "Smugglers use them, I shouldn't wonder. All those tunnels under the cliff! Dangerous, I call it. If the whole cliff doesn't fall down on Dover one fine day I'm a Dutchman."

"I'll take you down there one day, Becky," Milton promised teasingly. "Very romantic in the dark."

"Romantic!" She snorted, tossing her head.

He drained his beer, smacking his lips pleasurably. Taking a chair, he sat down, putting his feet up on the fire guard. "Ah, this is very relaxing! I like this house. Your Miss Rachel is the first of his females I've ever taken to."

"My Miss Rachel isn't anybody's female, I'll have you know. She is a lady, she is."

"Yes, I'll give you that. A real lady—anyone can see that. She speaks to you very nice and friendly. No airs or graces—but somehow you wouldn't overstep the mark. Dignity, that's what she's got. Some of them society women! Take Lady Danvers, for instance—real hellcat in private, she is. Snaps at her maid if she has the headache, throws hair brushes, stamps her feet. Not what I call a lady."

Becky nodded proudly. "Ah, Miss Rachel's as sweet as spice, never too proud to give a hand if one is needed, always open, always got her purse out if there's someone in the village needs a little extra. She makes no show, just does what has to be done quietly, without anyone seeing her. The new Vicar's wife will never be a patch on her. She's too bossy, too sharp-tongued. A little loving kindness goes further than any amount of money."

"Well, I hope we see her at the Park one day,"

Milton said. "There would be some glad faces, I can tell you!"

"I don't see her taking him," Becky said, on a faint sigh.

"What she got against him?" Milton demanded, insulted.

"All those females you was talking about, for a start. Do you think she wants to be one in a line? She has had offers enough in the past. When she was seventeen she was lovely enough to make your heart stand still. She could have married a dozen times over, but she said no to them all. She told me once; Becky, she said, when I marry it will be a man I can respect and love."

Milton was thoughtful. After a moment, he said, "Ah, but he's got a way with him. When a gentleman has charm it covers a lot of sins, and Mr. FitzCharles could charm the birds off the trees if he set his mind to it."

"I'd like to see him charm my Miss Rachel," Becky told him with a sniff. "She can be like granite when she thinks she's right."

The night passed without incident, and by morning the weather had cleared, and the sky was a sweet and tender blue, while the distant downs were softly wreathed in a pearly mist.

Peering from the kitchen window, Becky nodded. "Going to be a scorcher!"

Rachel looked up from her sewing. "Yes, it appears to promise well." She bent again over the sheet she was darning with tiny, immaculate stitches.

"You looked hipped this morning, Miss Rachel," said Becky in sturdy disapproval. "Why don't you keep to your bedroom for a few hours? You don't look as if you had any sleep last night."

"I am not so decayed that I am unable to do my accustomed tasks, Becky," Rachel said spiritedly. "I have told Christian he may get up and sit downstairs for an hour this morning. He is much recovered, do you not agree?"

Becky sniffed. "Oh, we are to have him all over the house now, are we? I hope, Miss, as you've warned Miss Lucy to stay out of his bedchamber from now on. It isn't right nor proper, her being alone with him up there."

"I have spoken to her," Rachel said crisply.

There was a loud knock on the door, and Becky opened it. She turned with a note in her hand. "From Mr. Freddy," she sniffed. "For Miss Amelia."

Rachel's brows rose in amused surprise. "Indeed?" She took the folded missive and went upstairs to Christian's room, where she found Amelia and Lucy playing cards with him.

When Rachel gave her the note, Amelia blushed and turned the small paper over and over in her hand, gazing at it as if it were a magic talisman.

"Open it, silly!" Lucy snapped, hovering impatiently.

"Yes, of course," gasped Amelia, her face scarlet. "I wonder what it can say?"

"If you do not open it we shall never know," Lucy said in sarcastic tones. Seeing that her sister was far too agitated to do anything sensible, she snatched the paper from her limp fingers and opened it.

"Give it back to me," Amelia wailed.

"Lucy, that was not very polite," said Rachel in dismay.

Lucy flung the note back at her sister. "It is an invitation from Freddy FitzCharles to drive with him to Dover to see the earthworks." She made a face at Christian. "Although why anyone should wish to do so I cannot imagine for they must be thoroughly boring."

Amelia was reading the brief note again and again. She looked up at Rachel excitedly. "May I go?"

"Certainly," Rachel said. "Lucy will accompany you."

"I do not wish to go," Lucy said in horror.

"Amelia must have a chaperone," Rachel insisted.

"Then you must go," Lucy said.

Christian gently urged her to please her sister by accompanying her. "After all, she has sat up here with us this morning for the same good reason," he pointed out.

"I wish to stay here with you," cried Lucy hotly. "It will be so dull, driving with Freddy, for he is the greatest bore in the world!"

"Oh, how can you say so? It is not true," cried Amelia, firing up at once.

Christian smiled wryly at Rachel over their heads. "I shall be quite happy reading a book, Lucy. I wish you to go. The fresh air will give you back some color. You have been looking pale these last two days."

Lucy capitulated at this endearing suggestion that he cared how she looked, and two girls went off, arguing as to what color each would wear.

Rachel sat down by Christian's side and gave him a searching glance. She was deeply concerned by Lucy's frank assertion of her wish to be with Christian. He looked at her calmly.

"You do not like to hear Lucy making plain her affection for me," he said gently.

"It is unfortunate," Rachel admitted.

"I understand," he nodded. "I am a Frenchman, an enemy of your country. It is impossible that Miss Lucy and I should ever marry, but I must tell you that I love her." He smiled. "I owe her my life. At first I was just grateful, but very quickly I fell in love with her pretty face, her impulsive nature, her unsophisticated warmth."

"She is still a child in many ways," Rachel said.

He nodded. "Yes, I know that. A trusting child. Do you think I would betray that trust?"

"Oh, I trust you, Christian," she said warmly. "I am only afraid that Lucy will be hurt by the inevitable parting."

"Do you have any notion of what Mr. Fitz-Charles means to do with me when he has caught his spy?" he asked.

"I am afraid it will mean Dover Castle until the war ends," she said regretfully.

"I suppose it would not be possible for me to have visitors while I am there?" he asked.

She smiled wryly. "Lucy?"

His face was wistful. "All I ask is a little hope, Miss Rachel. I do not ask for permission to speak to her, only that when the war ends I may return here, and if she is free to hear me, try to win her."

"My poor boy," she said. "There is so much between you, so many obstacles to happiness. You must not even think of it."

Lucy came running back into the room, wearing a pink-sprigged muslin and a straw bonnet tied with broad pink satin ribbons. She twirled around the room. "Will I do?" she demanded of Christian eagerly.

He shook his head teasingly at her. "Do not fish for compliments, Miss Lucy. Your mirror has already told you how pretty you look."

She gave him a dimpling, happy smile. "I wish that you could come with us! You would like to see Dover Harbor."

He laughed. "A Frenchman visiting one of your foremost naval harbors? My dear girl, I would be arrested in five seconds! Think how much military information I could find out there!"

"Oh, fiddle de dee," she said, tossing her head. "As if you would be interested in such prosy stuff!"

A short time later the carriage from the Park drew up outside the house, and Freddy leap out. Rachel walked with the two girls to the gate. She saw Sir Henry and Lady Danvers in the carriage beside Elizabeth Danvers. Mr. FitzCharles rode on Hercules beside the carriage. He raised his hat to her and asked if she were not to make a party.

"I thought you would also be coming?"

She shook her head. "I have a great deal to do in the house, thank you."

"I wish that you would change your mind," he urged.

The girls were safely settled beside Freddy, facing the Danvers family. Rachel saw Lady Danvers turn a cold and hostile eye towards her, and saw that, though she might be giving up Mr. FitzCharles from fear of exposure, she had not lost her jealous interest in him.

Stepping back, Rachel nodded at the coachman to drive on, and waved at her nieces in farewell. They waved back excitedly. Such excursions were rare in their lives, and Amelia, at least, meant to enjoy every second of it.

Mr. FitzCharles looked down at her, his hands loosely holding the reins against the great horse's mane.

"Be careful, then," he said roughly. "Remember, a hunted animal will be vicious in self-defense."

She looked at him, startled. "You think the spy may come again today?" Her cheeks lost some of their color. "Is this another of your traps?"

"What better opportunity for him than while we are all off to Dover?" He saw her anxious glance, and said, "Now, there is no cause for alarm this morning. He will not approach the house in daylight, but we have told him we shall dine late in Dover and return some time around nine. He may wait until dusk, hoping to steal through the park after the keepers have all gone home to supper."

"And Milton?" she asked.

"Milton will be with you this afternoon. I have given him orders to get here early. It is unlikely our friend will make his attempt before luncheon."

"I hope you may be right," she said.

"Rachel, please be very careful," he repeated in a husky tone. "I do not want to return to find I have lost you entirely."

She turned away, flushing, and muttered a hurried farewell before fleeing back into the house.

She found Christian in the parlor, wrapped in shawls upon the sofa, gazing in disbelief at the book of sermons Becky had given to help him while away the time.

Rachel laughed at his expression. "Becky wishes to improve your mind, I think."

"These are just the thing to send one to sleep," he said with feeling.

"Would you like me to sit here with you and talk, or shall you sleep?" she asked.

"If I read one of these I shall undoubtedly sleep," he said. "Pray, do not let me detain you, Rachel. I know how busy you are. Becky tells me you are to pickle onions today."

"Onions? No, no, she could not have said so. We are to make gooseberry jam."

She made her way to the kitchen, and at once plunged into feverish activity. There was so much to do that she quite forgot everything else, and it was not until the jam was all standing cooling, ready for potting, that she remembered Christian. "Poor fellow—he must be ravenous. It is half after twelve. Becky, have you some cold beef? I will take him a small repast to stay him until we have time to prepare something more substantial. His appetite is much improved today."

Becky grudgingly got the haunch of cold beef from the stone larder, carved some thin slices and heaped the plate with pickled walnuts, a pickled egg and some nasturtium seeds. "That should fill a corner or two for the present," she said.

"Thank you, Becky," Rachel said. She took the tray and went quietly down the passage to the parlor. She pushed the door open and went into the room. A sound behind her made her turn her head, casually. Then she froze.

Standing just on the threshold at her back was a masked figure, a drawn sword in his hand, his eyes glittering through the black velvet which hid his upper features.

Eleven

Shock hit her like a tidal wave. Her nerves jumped involuntarily, and she threw up the tray on which she carried Christian's meal, screaming Becky's name without even realizing what she did.

The intruder leapt back, his hand wavering so that the sword no longer pointed at her, cursing under his breath.

Then the kitchen door opened and Becky shot out, white-faced and instinctively calling Rachel's name.

"Do not move," the intruder hissed in a voice made unrecognizable by the peculiar way he spoke without opening his mouth. The sword quivered between them. "Either of you!"

Becky stood staring at him. "Heaven protect us," she moaned softly.

A sudden movement from the sofa drew the masked man's flickering eyes. He gestured to the two women to move into the room behind Rachel.

Christian sat up, staring, his face ashen. "Are you harmed, Miss Rachel?" he asked anxiously. "What did he do to you?"

"Nothing, nothing," she assured him. "Stay where you are, Christian. He cannot attack an unarmed man."

Christian laughed in bitter contempt. "That means nothing to such as him. He has no scruples about such small things. It is useless to appeal to his honor, Miss Rachel. Spies trade in most things, but never in honor."

"Your country was glad enough of my services," the man replied, in his strange, hoarse whisper.

"A pig is a useful animal," Christian said. "But one does not invite it into one's house."

The pale eyes glittered through the mask. The long mouth twisted. "I have come to dislike you, M'sieur Touslain. You have been a trouble to me. I shall enjoy ending your existence."

"No, no," Rachel cried in deep distress, moving so that she stood between him and sofa.

"No, Miss Rachel," Christian said in agitation, flinging back the shawls and jumping up.

"Out of the way," the spy whispered hoarsely, gesturing to Rachel. "I'll cut you to ribbons if you don't move!"

"I will not let you harm the poor boy," she said shakily, angry at a tendency in her legs to crumple beneath her.

Christian put a hand to her shoulder. "Move, Miss Rachel!" He grabbed a delicate, white-painted chair and held it before him, lunging at the spy with it.

The other swore viciously. With a deliberate, furious flick, he drew his sword up Rachel's arm, ripping her sleeve and leaving a long line of blood in his wake.

She felt a trail of fire along the passage of the wound. Becky screamed and pulled her back out of danger. "Oh, why did you do it? You might have been killed!"

"Are you much hurt, Miss Rachel?" Christian asked anxiously. He glared at the other man. "Canaille . . . to attack a woman!"

"Let her keep out of this business," the spy hissed. "Had she not harbored you, she would not have been harmed. Put down that chair, you fool. I can kill you any time I choose."

"Oh, yes, you have the advantage of me," Christian mocked. "But of this I am confident—you are afraid, and I am not!"

The spy darted forward, his sword slashing across the boys unprotected legs. Christian gasped. His chair was lowered as the cloth of his breeches tore, gaping to reveal an open wound.

The spy laughed. "Afraid, am I? We will see who is afraid, M'sieur. I will cut you piecemeal into ribbons." The sword lunged again, catching Christian on the unprotected shoulder. His shirt ripped. He gave a sharp cry of pain.

Christian half fell, half leapt backwards out of reach of the cruel silver blade. His voice was steady as he replied, "Canaille! You will never kill me."

The spy's white lips smiled. "Oh, yes, you have caused me such a vast deal of annoyance, you see. I shall squash you as I would an insect."

The sword flashed again, catching Christian on the back of the hand. Rachel sobbed, seeing his skin tear open, the blood drip down the delicate white chair.

"Insects can sting," Christian mocked him. "And this one is still alive to sting you again."

"I will soon alter that," the voice hissed. "I shall cut you into ribbons fine enough for this hospitable lady to wear on her best gown!"

Rachel's eye was caught by the fringed shawl flung to the floor by Christian when he rose. If she could reach it and throw it at the masked man it would blind him long enough for Christian to overpower him. She began slowly to edge her way towards it.

"Stand still, you stupid bitch," the spy hissed from the corner of his mouth. "Or I will lay open your silly face as I did your arm."

Rachel froze, watching him. After a moment he moved again, so suddenly that Christian was taken off guard. Backing, in momentary panic, Christian came up against the wall. The spy smiled that thin, cruel smile, his sword tip shooting forward in a flash of light.

Rachel threw herself on the shawl, ducked back and flung it over the spy's head. He had half turned, and seen her intention. The shawl fell, entangling his sword arm, but Rachel had followed her action with another, flinging herself at his knees, not to plead but to pull him down. He stumbled. Her fingers ripped agonizingly over his buckled shoes. He kicked out at her, catching her in the chest. She screamed, doubling up with pain, and heard through a darkness of agonizing pain the crash of glass as something came through the window.

Becky was crying somewhere above her. She could hear a heavy breathing, a sickening scrape of metal, then a familiar voice which made her heart leap with relief.

"James," she cried. "Oh, James. . . ."

Then Becky shrieked, and she opened her eyes, despite the pain which still held her, and saw the masked man holding Becky before him as a shield, backing away towards the passage.

"Keep still, all of you," the man hissed. "If you follow, I will kill her."

Rachel knelt up, staring at Becky with wide, wet eyes, trying desperately to convey to her an assurance that help would come. Becky's face was pale, but her mouth set grimly, and she looked back at her mistress with a comforting nod.

The door shut upon them. James stopped to lift her, holding her tightly against him, and she became oddly aware of the strength hidden beneath the languid elegance of his fashionable clothes.

"Rachel, my dearest love, are you much hurt? What did that swine do to you? There is blood on your dress and you are so white . . . I shall never forgive myself for letting this happen to you. I miscalculated again—I underestimated the strength of his desire to be rid of the threat to his safety."

"Better late then never," Christian said. "Is not that what you say in England? I know, now, what you mean! Mon Dieu, but I was glad to see you come through that window."

Rachel looked imploringly at Mr. FitzCharles. "Becky," she said. "Please, do something. . . ."

James smiled, dropped a kiss lightly on the top of her head, and said, "My dearest girl, do you imagine I would be standing here chatting if I had not made arrangements to stop all the holes? Milton is outside, waiting for the fellow."

She sagged in relief, and he supported her. "Bear up, my dear—not much longer."

She looked at Christian, saw that he was white to the very lips, and exclaimed in self-disgust. "Oh, poor boy, and I had forgot you! I must see to those dreadful wounds!"

Christian grinned. "They are scratches, I assure you. My dear FitzCharles, may we not go out now and see what is happening? I feel like someone who is missing the last battle of a war."

Mr. FitzCharles examined his face carefully. "Do you think you are up to walking so far?"

Christian shrugged. "My curiosity will overweigh any pain from these scratches."

They found Milton seated on a rustic seat beneath an apple tree, a gun across his knees, looking cheerful and relaxed.

The masked man faced him, Becky still held as a living shield. When they appeared, the eyes, the only alive part of his hiden face, shifted to take them into account.

"Inefficient," remarked Mr. FitzCharles in light sneering tones. "I had thought you capable of better things. You have twice bungled the business."

"Women must always ruin one's caluculations," the other retorted in the same languid voice.

"How true," Mr. FitzCharles sighed.

"But for once I shall use them for my own purposes," the spy went on softly. "I am leaving here, and this woman goes with me. Her life depends upon mine. If I am threatened, I shall kill her without hesitation."

"You cannot take her far," observed Mr. FitzCharles. "She is a very temporary hostage. Sooner or later you will be seized, and then begins the sickening business of a trial; imprisonment in a foul dungeon, uncleanliness, crude companions, the misery of hearing your crimes listed for the world to understand. After that a short wait and a shorter walk. Then the final, degrading spectacle—a public execution."

The masked man seemed to shiver as he listened, passing his tongue over his pallid lips.

Softly, Mr. FitzCharles said, "You can escape all that, my dear man. Let the woman go."

The glittering eyes stared at him intently. "And then?"

Mr. FitzCharles unsheathed the sword stick he carried. The sunlight danced along the blade edge, dazzling Rachel's eyes. She began to tremble.

The masked man laughed and pushed Becky from him, crouching in readiness for the attack.

Their swords flashed, ribbons of shining light, crossing and flickering, dazzling her so that she could not follow properly what was happening.

She had never seen men fight like this, the swords hissing in the air like snakes, seeming to twine together in loving embrace then separate, to flash and cut down, to leap forward and through with deadly rapidity. The eye could barely follow their swift movements or determine which had the advantage.

Mr. FitzCharles fought with intense concentration, his facial muscles tense.

"You seem surprised by my skill, sir," the masked man panted. "But then you have always underestimated me."

"Why, yes, I see I did," drawled Mr. FitzCharles. "I admit you have surprised me of late." His wrist flicked, the long blade of the sword sneaked under the other's guard and he gave a stifled cry of pain as the point found a mark.

"It is a mistake to talk," Mr. FitzCharles murmured. "One loses concentration."

His opponent did not answer. He was fighting desperately, perspiration becoming visible along the top of the black mask and soaking downwards. His tongue passed over his lips continually, as if he were dry-mouthed. Once Rachel saw his throat move convulsively at a deadly thrust from Mr. FitzCharles, and the hand holding his sword shook even before he parried, clenching so hard that the knuckles showed white.

Becky and Rachel clung together, as silent and intent as the duelists themselves. Rachel felt that she would not recognize herself if she were to catch sight of her own reflection at this moment. Emotions she had never known before filled her entirely. Pity, terror, rage engulfed her.

The masked figure was losing ground now. The arm holding his sword seemed almost to find it too heavy. There was an air of deadly resignation growing about him.

Mr. FitzCharles was pressing him harder, his sword blade seemingly irresistible. Then with a suddenness that sent her heart leaping into her mouth, his foot slipped on the damp grass and he fell forward just as Mr. FitzCharles's sword flashed forward in a lunge.

There was a choked, bubbling cry of anguish. He faltered in his step, stood for a second, his hands going to his chest, hen crumpled, coughing, a gush of blood coming from his lips.

Rachel stood, tears running down her face, watching him in an agonized pity.

He fell like a tree cut down by an axeman. James stared down at him, then knelt and looked closely. The others moved slowly forward in time to see him strip the small piece of black velvet from the white face.

"He is dead," Mr. FitzCharles said heavily.

Rachel gasped. "It is Mr. Brown!"

"I guessed it might be," James murmured. "His position as my secretary made it possible, and his private circumstances made it likely. He had no private income, yet he dressed far too well and gambled heavily in London. I tried to give him a hint that I suspected him. I hoped he might flee the country. But he was a gambler. He preferred to stay and risk exposure on the hope that he could silence Touslain."

Rachel stared down at the dead man's livid face. The image of his death haunted her. It came and went in blurs of light. Her legs felt suddenly very weak beneath her.

She did not know that all color had left her face, nor that she was trembling as though in the grip of an ague.

Her eyes closed against the spinning of the light, and then everything fell away, whirring and rushing, as though in a great wind, taking her with it.

Twelve

She opened her eyes to find herself lying upon the sofa in the parlor. Mr. FitzCharles knelt beside her, watching her with a curiously intent expression in his gray eyes, like a cat at a mousehole.

Color flooded into her cheeks. She tried to sit up, and he pressed her shoulders down upon the cushions. As she lay back, she remembered, and her lips trembled.

"I did not dream it. He . . . he is dead."

"Quite dead," he said gently. "Do not look so sad, my dear. It is really better so—for him."

She swallowed, her mind carrying the image of that white face, the bloody lips and staring eyes. "I . . . I never saw a man die so before."

"It is something you forget," he agreed calmly.

She closed her eyes for a moment. Then, "Where is Becky?"

"I have sent her to fetch you a glass of that infernal elderflower wine of hers—you are in need of a stimulant and there is nothing else that will serve." His smile was wry.

She shivered, realizing how cold she was, with a deathly coldness that had invaded her when she fainted, and had not yet passed away. He drew a rug over her with gentle hands.

"You are suffering from shock," he told her.

"I shall be very well in a moment," she assured him.

His eye fell upon her ripped sleeve, stiff with dried blood, and his face darkened. "For that alone he deserved to die! It was a piece of damnable cowardice to hurt a woman so!"

Becky bustled in with a tray on which stood a glass of her wine, a bowl of steaming water and some torn rags. She looked sharply at Rachel, and muttered at the sight of her white face.

"Becky, how is Christian?" Rachel asked anxiously.

"I have dealt with his wounds," Becky nodded. "I put him back to bed just now. He will survive! That young man is as tough as a piece of shoe leather."

She lifted Rachel's head and made her drink the wine, then gently sponged her arm, tearing back the material to expose the scratch.

"I hope that you will have no scar," she said crossly. "You should not have come between them!"

"I had to do something," Rachel said, half apologetically. "I could not stand by and see him kill poor Christian, could I?" She glanced at Mr. FitzCharles. "How did you come to be there so opportunely? I had thought you many miles away."

"Just what I intended Brown to think. It was another trap, and this time the mouse came forth, very carefully, and seeing no sign of any trap put his head inside after the cheese. Then . . . snap!"

She shuddered. "Poor man!"

Becky looked at her indignantly. "Poor man, indeed! After he tried to kill all of us? I am very glad he is dead."

Mr. FitzCharles laughed. "Becky is right. Such pity does your heart much credit, but your mind none at all. He was a traitor, a murderer and a rascal with little conscience or scruple."

"You were sorry for him yourself," she said quietly.

He sighed. "I was. Yes. I wish I had taken better precautions than I did, however. To tell the truth I never anticipated an attack upon this house in broad daylight—even though I had made it possible and was waiting for him. He had more audacity and courage than I had thought. I wish you had not paid the price of my folly, Rachel—had I not wanted to make certain my trap closed on him you need never have suffered as you did. I blame myself."

"Oh, no," she said softly, smiling at him.

"I wished to make certain his guilt was proved," he explained. "The only way was to catch him redhanded. I was prepared to risk Touslain's life, but that I should have risked yours is something I shall never forgive myself for—you might so easily have been killed. I had not believed him capable of that. I had thought your sex would protect you. I was wrong. He was totally without scruple."

Becky bridled. "All this for a Frenchman!"

Rachel frowned at her affectionately. "Take away the tray, Becky. This bandage will do."

"You must rest now," Becky said, glaring at Mr. FitzCharles. "You must leave, sir."

He rose to his feet, smiling down at Rachel with a tenderness that warmed her heart. "I will see you tomorrow, my dear. May I call on you in the morning?"

At that moment Lucy burst into the room and came to a standstill, her eyes moving around, taking in Rachel's bandaged arm and white face, the white chair thrown in the corner, the blood stains on the carpet beside the sofa.

She screamed, her hand clutching her bodice. "Christian! Oh, good God, what has happened?"

"There is no need for hysterics, "Miss," observed Mr. FitzCharles lazily. "He is perfectly safe upstairs."

Lucy sighed with relief. "But then why is Rachel's arm bandaged?" she demanded, poised for flight to Christian's side.

"I wondered when you would express concern for your aunt rather than screeching like a peahen over a young man," Mr. FitzCharles said drily.

Amelia was in the doorway, her eyes wide. "Oh, Rachel, what has happened to you?"

"We had a visitor," said Mr. FitzCharles, smiling at Rachel.

Amelia ran to the sofa and flung herself down beside her aunt. "Dearest Rachel, are you much hurt?"

"You can see she is not," Lucy said.

"Yes, it is a scratch, the merest scratch," Rachel dismissed easily.

Amelia shrieked. "Do not say that while we were gone the spy attacked you?"

Freddy had sauntered in, somewhat bewildered, but at Amelia's words his face darkened with angry suspicion. "Spy? James, what is this? What have you been keeping from me?"

Mr. FitzCharles laughed. "We must not stand here talking while Miss Rachel is wanting to have some much-needed rest," he said.

Lucy, however, took pity on Freddy, and eagerly sketched the whole story for him, while Mr. FitzCharles watched with amusement.

"Well," declared Freddy, highly indignant that he had been excluded from this excitement, "I do think it too bad of you, James. I knew that there was something afoot when you kept coming down here, but I thought that . . ." He came to a full stop, looking conscious. "Well, I misunderstood your motive." He gave Rachel a silly smile, then flung a scowl at his brother. "You might have given me a hint, you know!"

"How could I know you were not the spy?" Mr. FitzCharles said, tongue in cheek.

Freddy looked first astounded, then furious. "I? A spy? Damn it, what do you mean?" Then, seeing his brother's twinkling eyes he began to laugh and punched him playfully on the shoulder. "Oh, it is your little joke, James! I do not think that so very amusing, I can tell you! And I shall not soon forgive you for keeping me out of all the fun."

"I do not think you missed much," Rachel told him. "I found it extremely unpleasant."

Freddy looked pityingly at her. "Yes, for you it must have been, Ma'am. I can see that. Ladies do not like such things. But I dare say James enjoyed it well enough."

"Oh, no!" cried Rachel, much distressed. "To kill another human creature! How could he?"

"It was not the way I should have chosen, had there been any alternative," Mr. FitzCharles agreed gravely.

"But who was the spy?" Amelia asked innocently.

"My secretary, Brown," she was informed. Lucy gave a shriek of disgust.

"What, that little sneaking fellow? I should not have believed it. Well, I was never so let down in my life. He was a nobody! Are you certain it was he?"

Mr. FitzCharles smiled. "His quiet manner cloaked a great deal which would shock you, Miss Lucy."

"I never liked him," Freddy said. "Queer sort of fellow, had a way of creeping up behind you when you were talking which was damned ill-bred. Had you told me what was in the wind, James, I'd have said like a shot—Brown, that is your man!" Filled with the euphoria of hindsight he gazed reproachfully at his brother. "You would do better to consult me next time."

"Next time," exclaimed Rachel, revolted.

Mr. FitzCharles gave her an amused glance. "Should such an opportunity ever occur, which for the sake of Rachel's sanity, we must hope it will not—I promise to consult you, Freddy."

"Did he have access to truly important information?" she asked him soberly.

"I cannot be certain until I have checked, but he was my private secretary, you know, and did not work on state papers. Such information as he gained must have been from listening to private conversation."

"What did I tell you!" cried Freddy.

"The trouble is," his brother added thoughtfully, "London is full of French agents at present, trying to discover exactly what terms we are prepared to accept in the hope of making a treaty. You can see how valuable this would be to Bonaparte—he would be playing for high stakes knowing precisely which cards we held, and able to trump our aces."

Freddy was frowning. "I say, James," he burst

out. "If we search his papers we may find the names of a dozen other agents!"

Mr. FitzCharles smiled lazily at him. "You would have me search them, I suppose! His papers will be sealed and sent to London to be examined by persons more skilled in such matters than I. I am not qualified to take up the profession of spy-catcher."

Freddy looked disappointed.

His brother smiled at him. "I had a personal interest in catching him—it is not every day one finds oneself being used as a cloak for such activities. I was angry that my name had been used as a cover for spying. It was a matter of personal pride."

"I do not understand," said Rachel to Lucy, "why you are back from Dover so early? I had thought you would not be back until it was dark?"

"I wished it to be thought that this was the case," said Mr. FitzCharles. "When I left them, a mile past the village, I told Freddy he need not hurry. I hoped they would take their time."

"Lucy fidgeted so much we could not enjoy a moment of it," Amelia said crossly. "She was very tedious."

Rachel eyed Lucy critically, and was glad to see her blush and look ashamed. The strain of the day was beginning to tell upon Rachel, though. She yawned, and Mr. FitzCharles said, "We must take our leave. You will wish to rest." He bowed over her hand, kissing it lightly. "Shall we have the pleasure of your presence at dinner tomorrow? Sir Henry and his wife are leaving us tomorrow morning. We shall be a small party. You need not feel constrained by a need to put on a society face. It will be a quiet evening."

"Thank you," she said. "I should be glad to dine with you."

Lucy and Amelia stared at each other, suddenly aware of something they had not noticed until this moment—there was an intimate air between their aunt and Mr. FitzCharles which astonished them. Amelia merely noticed it with puzzled surprise. Lucy, always quicker, began to put two and two together, and make a very startling discovery.

When they were in their room alone, Lucy confided her new notion to Amelia, and was given a look of incredulous dismay.

"Rachel and James FitzCharles! Lucy, what foolishness. It is laughable."

"Much you know," Lucy said stalwartly. "Well, we must wait and see, but I should not dislike to live at the Park, for my part."

"Rachel does not even like him," Amelia cried. "Think what she has always said of him!"

"I know," Lucy said. "But I saw how they looked at one another just now, and I do not give a fig for what she *said*. She is in love."

The following evening, Lucy begged permission to stay at home instead of making one of the party going to the Park. Since Rachel knew that Christian would not long be left free she turned a blind eye to Lucy's reason, and gave her leave to sit up in the parlor for an hour or two, playing cards with Christian under Becky's watchful eye.

Mr. FitzCharles sent his carriage for Rachel and Amelia, and welcomed them warmly when they were announced. His mother sat on the sofa, between George and Elizabeth, turning the pages of an album of family sketches. Freddy came forward eagerly to greet Amelia, taking her off to a corner of the room to talk about their trip to Dover, and excitedly recalling the part of the tunnels which had special provision for the pouring of boiling oil over any attackers. This medieval relic had taken Freddy's fancy. Rachel heard him declare, "I cannot think why it is not used today."

Mr. FitzCharles looked at Rachel, a smile in his eyes. "Freddy is very bloodthirsty! I have just received a parcel of books from town—some new novels among them. Will you look at them? They are in the library."

She felt her cheeks grow hot. His true intention was barely disguised, and she did not know quite how to respond. In these last few days events had moved so fast, her own feelings had become so much clearer to her in the heightened atmosphere of danger in which they had all been living.

He extended his arm, the elbow crooked to receive her hand. She hesitated, then sighed, and placed her fingertips upon his sleeve.

As they left the drawing room, Mrs. FitzCharles looked after them with anxious, hopeful eyes. Elizabeth, watching her, saw how strained were her features, and laid a hand on hers.

Mrs. FitzCharles started. When she glanced round Elizabeth smiled gently. "I think mine will not be the only wedding in this family, Ma'am. You must be very happy."

Mrs. FitzCharles smiled back at her. "It is the wish of my heart to see him settled. I want to have grandchildren running around these rooms."

George shivered. "You females will go on so fast! Why speak of children before the wedding knot is tied!"

Elizabeth scolded him tenderly, and he laughed,

content to have her treat him as a child for as long as might be. Mrs. FitzCharles, observing this, wondered if it might not be the case that George had felt deprived of a mother's love for so long that he wished for that from his wife rather than any more demanding emotion. But, seeing Elizabeth's happy smile, she shrugged. What did it matter, so long as both of them were happy?

Mr. FitzCharles spread the books out upon the table, and Rachel bent over them with a fast-beating heart. She picked one up and flicked over the pages idly.

He watched her averted profile. "Rachel, you must know what I wish to ask you. I have spoken to you on the same theme before, but then we did not know each other well enough. I hope that we have lately come to know each other better. I feel that I know you in a way I never did before. If the subject is too distasteful to you, still, I will not go on, but if I may at least hope that you will listen to me with any sort of sympathy, then . . ." He stammered to a halt, spreading his hands in a gesture that finished his sentence for him.

Her shaking fingers still pretended to turn the pages of books she could hardly see. A haze clouded her vision, and her pulse seemed to deafen her. "I . . ." She tried to speak, but failed miserably.

"I am thinking of giving up my career, and settling here at the Park," he offered hurriedly. "You would not need to alter your way of life so very much, Rachel. I know you dislike London. . . ."

Rachel felt a sudden wave of joy sweep her. She

straightened and looked at him with dancing amusement. "A reformed man, sir?"

His face changed, grew radiant with hope. "Are you laughing at me? I swear to you, I am ready to change my whole way of life for you. Do you want me to be as sober as a judge? I shall touch no strong wine without your leave. Do you want me to join the Methodists? I may even do that!"

"You mock me, sir," she said reprovingly. "This is a fine beginning!"

He laughed, taking her hand. "Oh, I could walk on my head, I do believe, or eat fire, like a fellow at a circus—I am over the moon and ocean-deep in love, my dearest girl."

"And will give up all others of my sex?" she asked, half seriously. "I do not think, James, that I could bear to suffer the pangs of jealousy. When I heard from Lucy that Lady Danvers had been with you at the Temple, I suffered then, most bitterly—I would not wish to feel so again."

His face was serious, the dark head bent over her hand, his mouth hot against her cool skin. "I did not escape that pit, my dear—you do not know how close I came to throttling that dreadful Master Mellows for his impudence in proposing to you! It was then that I knew I could never rest until you were my wife, however long I had to wait, however hard you resisted."

She gave a harsh sigh. "For me the moment of realization came when you were fighting poor Mr. Brown. That you might be killed was so intolerable a thought that I knew I must love you beyond belief."

His face grew taut with passion. He took her by the shoulders, looking down into her features with brooding eyes. "You love me," he murmured thickly.

Her mouth trembled. "James, yes," she whispered, overcome with sudden shyness.

She heard his sharp intake of breath. He caught her up in hard arms, his lips seeking hers. The violent release of feeling which followed told her how deeply he had invaded her heart. She sighed against his kiss, and her arms crept up around his neck.

He moved slightly away so that he could look at her. His eyes ran over the cloudy eyes, the upturned parted mouth, the slightly smiling look of pleasure which remained upon her face from his kiss.

He closed his eyes briefly, and then looked at her again. "Yes," he murmured, "yes, now I believe you love me. Oh, Rachel, I will be a very possessive husband, jealous and passionate. I know the follies and temptations of married women. You shall never be exposed to them. I shall haunt you like the ghost of Hamlet's father. You shall be cherished, cosseted, adored."

She laughed, a twinkle coming into her eyes. "For the first week, perhaps, sir. But what then?"

He shook his head. "I am serious. London will blink at the transformation. The rake, the gamester gone—in their place the married man! A modern miracle." His eyes danced.

"Do not change too much," she said, touching his cheek. "I find I love you very well as you are. I fought against loving you so long that I have fairly worn out all my prejudices against you. All that is left is a core of delight that you exist."

His face grew intent, he stroked her hair. "I should have said that to you, my dear. You are my delight, and when you say my name my pulses leap with joy."

She put a hand to the nape of his neck. His breath caught violently. "My love," he groaned, pulling her closer, his head bending to hers.

Rachel surrendered to the passionate urgency of his kiss, her arms clinging to his neck. Suddenly the door behind them was flung open. They leapt apart and turned to find Freddy staring at them, his face a picture of astonishment and embarrassment.

"You come just in time to congratulate me, Freddy," James said, grinning at his brother's expression. "Allow me to present to you the future mistress of FitzCharles Park, and your future sister in law."

Freddy's jaw dropped. "Good God," he said. "Good God."